Earl B. Pilgrim

BEYOND
THE CALL

Tales from Baxter Gillard

ii

Earl B. Pilgrim

DRC PUBLISHING

3 Parliament Street
St. John's, Newfoundland and Labrador
A1A 2Y6
Telephone: (709) 726-0960
E-mail: info@drcpublishingnl.com
www.drcpublishingnl.com

Library and Archives Canada Cataloguing in Publication

Pilgrim, Earl B. (Earl Baxter), 1939-
Beyond the call / Earl B. Pilgrim.

ISBN 978-1-926689-09-8

1. Newfoundland and Labrador--Fiction. I. Title.

PS8581.I338B49 2009   C813'.54   C2009-903950-8

Layout and design by Becky Pendergast
Cover design by Jessica Penney

Published 2010
Printed in Canada

Table of Contents

Dedicated to

Wilson Canning (July 18,1933-August 1, 2009)
Adopted and raised by Mae and Walter Canning of Roddickton,
he spent most of his life in St. John's working in real estate
and as a city bus driver. Wilson had a great passion for music.

In memory

Baxter Gillard (1903-2002) was born in Englee, Canada Bay and
educated at the Methodist Church School in that community. He
joined the firm of John Reeves in 1925 and worked there until his
retirement in 1977. In 1948, he helped to plan and organize a town
council for Englee. He was appointed Deputy Mayor in 1950 and
Mayor in 1953, a post he held continually until 1982. Gillard was
active in the community and also in church affairs, holding several
offices, including Chairman and Secretary-Treasurer of the United
Church Board of Education in Englee from 1944 to 1970 and
Secretary-Treasurer of the United Church Board of Trustees from
1927 to 1969. Gillard received several awards in recognition of his
contribution to the community. In 1971 the Newfoundland and
Labrador Federation of Municipalities presented him with a
Testimonial of Appreciation. The United Church Conference
awarded him a Certificate of Appreciation in 1980 and in 1981
Memorial University of Newfoundland bestowed an honorary
Doctor of Laws degree on him. (information, courtesy
Encyclopedia of Newfoundland and Labrador)

The Picture on the Wall

CHAPTER
1

One evening I visited the home of eighty-six-year-old Dr. Baxter T. Gillard in Englee, Newfoundland. It was obvious he had been reading for quite some time because his eyes were red and watering. After I said good evening, he invited me into the kitchen to have a cup of strong, steeped tea, saying in his deep bass voice that it was better out there because we were closer to the kettle and could talk more comfortably sitting at the table. Dr. Gillard was an important man. In October 1981, he received an honourary doctor of laws from Memorial University of Newfoundland and Labrador for being the mayor of his hometown of Englee for more than thirty years and a lay reader with the United Church of Canada for close to half a century.

On this evening, as we sat at the table reminiscing I noticed a peculiar picture hanging on the wall across from me. The picture was framed and covered with glass but it looked old and I was sure it had seen better days. It was wrinkled and slightly faded.

"That's an old picture, Mr. Gillard," I said.

"Yes, it's over a hundred years old. I knew the man who drew it," he said.

"Go on!" I said with interest.

"While the kettle is boiling I'll tell you the story about that picture and how it came about," he said.

****

It was just before the turn of the century when a young man by the name of Philaenus (Phil) Reeves was getting ready to leave home in Canada Harbour. Phil told his parents he was going away to seek his fortune. He said he wasn't going to hang around fishing boats any more. He said he was a man, almost sixteen, and had yet to see his first dollar so he was leaving home. His father looked at him and asked where he would go. Phil said he didn't care where he went. He just wanted to make his own money and see the world. He said he was going to go to St. John's and get a ride on the first schooner that would take him. His father, Pat, was torn to the heart. He knew his son was high strung and was concerned he would get into trouble. 'You don't have a cent of money and I don't have any to give you, what do you think you will live on?' he asked.

'I don't care what I'll live on. I'll eat grass like a goat if I have to. I'm just not staying here working for nothing any longer,' said Phil.

Phil's father knew he was right, he himself had fished now for twenty years and never broke even. There was silence in the kitchen as Phil's mother, Rose, took pans of bread from the oven. She held up a fresh loaf and said, 'Won't you miss this, Phil?'

'You know I'll miss it, Mother, it's the best bread in the world, but a loaf of bread is not enough,' Phil said. Phil Reeves was a smart lad; people who knew him said he was never stuck for a word. Now, he turned to his mother and said with a grin, 'Mom, doesn't it say somewhere in the good book that a young man like me cannot live on bread alone, not even the loaf you just took out of the oven.'

Even though she wasn't happy to hear Phil say he was leaving home, his mother had to laugh. 'I'll miss you if you go away,' she said.

'Mom, I want you to pack my clothes. I'm going on the first boat heading out of here, tonight if I can,' he told her. With that, he went outside. After Phil left the kitchen, Rose started crying She knew it was impossible to keep her son at home in Canada Harbour. He had made up his mind to leave and that was it.

'Where do you think he will go?' she asked her husband.

'I don't know,' Pat said. 'If he goes to St. John's I suppose he can stay with my brother Leo until he finds a job. But we'll have to give him a letter telling Leo who he is, because Leo hasn't seen him since he was a small boy.'

Pat sat and stared at the floor, wondering if there was anything else he could do to keep his son at home. He knew he had nothing to offer him, he hadn't seen a dollar in years. But he finally said he wasn't going to let Phil leave without some money in his pocket.

'What do you mean by that, Pat?' asked Rose.

'Joe Stuckless (the fish merchant) owes me money, you know that,' he said.

'There's not much you can do about it unless you commit murder,' Rose said.

'I'm having some of that money today to give to Phil. If not, there will be bloodshed in Canada Harbour,' Pat said as he struck his fist on the table.

'Listen Pat, don't you go over there and kick up a fuss. Joe is the justice of the peace. He can have the magistrate come and throw you in the clink,' said Rose.

'I don't care about the magistrate or anyone else. Phil is leaving home and I want a ten dollar bill to give him, and I'm having it,' said Pat, as he put on his coat and went out the door.

Rose knew when Pat got mad he was capable of creating trouble. There was only so much, though, a man could put up with before he was forced to stand up for his rights. She had seen it before when they lived in Harbour Grace, Conception Bay, and that was the reason they had come north to Canada Harbour. Rose shuddered as she recalled what happened in Harbour Grace on Boxing Day 1883. In an awful incident known as the Harbour Grace Affray, ongoing hostility between Protestants and Roman Catholics resulted in a confrontation that left five dead and 17 injured. That time, hot tempered Pat was lucky he hadn't got himself and his younger brother killed.

Rose went to the door and yelled, 'Now Pat, listen, it's better to be sensible about this, we'll get money somewhere for Phil. It's not worth making a fuss.'

****

Sometime later, Phil Reeves boarded a fishing schooner laden with salt cod. It had come in to take shelter from a northwest gale. It was heading to Conception Bay after a summer fishing on the Labrador. Phil felt rich as he jingled the money in his pocket, ten one dollar coins. His father had made Joe Stuckless cough up the money. They must have had a racket because when his father returned to the house he had some buttons missing from the front of his shirt. But Phil didn't care, he was heading out.

It was a rough trip going to Bay Roberts, Conception Bay. On two occasions the skipper thought the small vessel would be lost. Once, they nearly crashed into the cliffs.

When they arrived in Bay Roberts the schooner had part of her railing missing and most of the canvas was stripped from the masts.

'I've never experienced a storm like that before,' the captain said. 'Maybe the young passenger brought us bad luck. Anyway, we made it home. But we won't let him go on to St. John's with us tomorrow.'

Phil asked the skipper what he charged for the trip. 'Nothing, glad to get rid of you, hope you have better luck,' the skipper said.

Phil walked along the busy Bay Roberts waterfront. There were about ten schooners by the wharf. Some were loading lumber, others were loading dried cod to take to markets as far away as Spain. After just getting off that 'sinking tub' as he called it, Phil wasn't one bit interested in getting on another ship, especially one going across the Atlantic Ocean. He inquired about the mail steamer going to St. John's and was told it wouldn't arrive for a week.

'Are you looking for a job, son?' inquired a man who had noticed Phil standing near a pile of salt dry fish.

'Yes sir I am,' he replied.

'Then you can put down your bag and start right away.'

'Okay sir, what do you want me to do?' Phil asked.

'You and that other young fellow over there can start carrying fish to the weights on a hand-barrow.' The man pointed to a stack of hand-barrows near a shed. 'I'll pay you fifteen cents an hour, but you have to work ten hour days. There's at least ten days work here.'

Phil was delighted. He saw where he could make fifteen dollars or more. The man suggested a boarding house and Phil started work right away. Phil Reeves was a hard worker; anyone who had him in their employ was more than pleased with his work. He was a jack of all trades, able to do anything he was asked to do. He worked for over a month helping to load salt bulk fish on board schooners, getting paid a dollar and a half every day. He hardly knew how to count the money, he was making so much. One day, the merchant came and asked Phil if he wanted to accompany the loaded schooner to St. John's to help with the offloading. Phil said that was where he was heading in the first place. Maybe now he would get to see his Uncle Leo.

'I want my pay before I go, sir,' he told the merchant.

'That won't be a problem,' the merchant replied. 'You earned your pay. You can have it before the schooner leaves.'

The merchant paid Phil sixty dollars for forty days work and Phil thought he was a millionaire. He had never dreamed there was so much money in the world.

'If Dad could only see me now,' he said as he walked to the house where he was paying thirty cents a day for his board. He gave his landlady twelve dollars and counted the remaining forty-eight dollars several times before putting it safely in his pocket. 'I am leaving in the morning, going to St. John's with the schooner to help off-load, should be back in four days,' he told the landlady.

'I doubt if you'll ever be back again,' she told him. 'But, anytime you happen to be this way and want a boarding house, our door will always be open to you.'

Phil thanked her and went to pack his clothes. At 5 a.m. the next morning, he boarded the schooner and left Bay Roberts, never to return again.

****

Phil was a very excited young man as the schooner started reefing the canvas going through the narrows of St.

John's Harbour. He was entering the capital city of Newfoundland he had heard his father talk so much about. His father hadn't wanted to leave the city, but he didn't have much choice due to his involvement with the Harbour Grace Affray. After that incident, he was given two options, either get out and head for the Northern Peninsula or stay and put up with the consequences. He chose to head out.

Phil saw a great many schooners and ships tied to the docks around the harbour; some were the biggest he had ever seen and he just stood and stared. The crew had a night off before the offloading started the next day, a job that would take about ten hours. Phil decided this was a good time to visit his Uncle Leo. He took his clothes bag with him and told one of the men where he intended to go.

'If I don't show up early tomorrow morning you'll know where I am,' he said.

Phil walked from Bowring's wharf onto Water Street. He had seen cars in Bay Roberts but not like this, they were everywhere. He went into one of the many stores and managed to get directions to his uncle's house. Leo lived in the west end of St. John's, about a forty-five minute walk from Bowring's wharf. Phil wondered what his uncle would say when he saw him. Would he welcome him into his home or turn him away? He didn't know.

It was twilight when Phil arrived at his uncle's house. The door was opened by a young girl close to Phil's age. She had red hair and a freckled face and looked like his sister, who was three years older than him.

'Is this the home of Mr. Leo Reeves?' he politely asked.

'Yes sir, it is. Would you like to see him?' she asked.

'Yes please,' he stammered.

'Just a moment,' she said and then turned away to call.

'Dad, Dad, someone is here to see you.'

In less than a minute Phil found himself standing in front of a tall man who looked like his father's twin.

'Yes, young man, what can I do for ya?' he asked.

'I'm Phil Reeves, Pat's son from Canada Harbour.'

Leo Reeves had not forgotten his brother Pat and what he had done for him. It was Pat's taking the blame for their part in the Harbour Grace Affray that had allowed Leo to stay in St. John's. He had tried many times to get Pat to come back to the city but Pat was afraid. Leo held out both arms and embraced Phil like a son as he invited him inside and introduced him to his wife, Joan, and their two daughters.

'You're as welcome as the flowers in spring to this house, my boy,' said his uncle.

Phil thanked him; he knew his uncle meant it. The conversation centered on Paddy. Leo had not seen his brother since he left St. John's more than twenty years ago.

'How and when did you get here, me boy?' asked Leo.

'I came this morning on a schooner laden with salt cod. We're tied up at Bowring's wharf. It took us all day to unload. Tomorrow, the schooner takes on a load of freight and heads back to Bay Roberts,' said Phil.

'You can stay here with us tonight and for as long as you want,' said Leo.

'I am not going back to Bay Roberts on the return trip. I will help load the schooner tomorrow, then I am going to try to get a job in the city,' said Phil.

'I know where ya can get work, son, there's lots of jobs around and they pay cash too,' said Leo.

Phil dug out the letter from his father. Leo opened the envelope and read the letter with tears in his eyes. 'So you have decided not to become a fisherman,' he said. 'Your father says you're going to try and make a living on the land.'

'I don't know if I'll be able to make a living on the land or at sea, but I am not going to work in a fishing boat and be at the mercy of a fish merchant,' said Phil.

****

Within a day or two Phil went to work with a shipping company that loaded vessels with freight going to ports all over Newfoundland and Labrador. This work continued until the middle of December when the boats stopped running due to winter freeze up. The company then usually sent some of their employees to the United States to do the same work in various ports along the eastern seaboard. The company manager called Phil in to ask if he wanted to go to work in New York, doing the same as he was doing in St. John's.

'You'll get paid more money and have free board and lodging. Pay is forty cents an hour. You should do well down there.'

Phil was interested in the offer. It would be a lot better than getting laid off and having to look for another job. He asked for a day to think about the offer and was given until noon the following day. That night he talked to his Uncle Leo who encouraged him to take the job, saying it was a great opportunity and he should give it a try for the winter months at least. Two days later, when the five-master *Douglas Pearl* pushed away from the docks in St. John's, Phil was on board bound for New York.

CHAPTER
2

The voyage to New York was hard for the sixteen-year-old Newfoundlander. He was belittled by a very rowdy crew of mostly ex-naval seamen. The captain didn't allow any liquor and Phil later said if there had been any drinking aboard someone would have been killed for sure. The sailors wrestled and fought. Several fights broke out while they were gambling which caused the captain to come below and threaten to go into the nearest port and throw everyone off. Phil sat in the shadows and took it all in; it was the greatest education of his life.

Four days after leaving St. John's, the *Douglas Pearl* sailed into New York and was towed to her berth. Phil and the four Newfoundlanders with him were happy to get off the ship and begin work on the New York waterfront.

A month later, fed up with pushing loaded trolley carts onto ships bound for ports around the world, Phil decided to look for a job away from the docks. The foreman liked Phil; he was a hard worker and very strong. He said he knew where Phil could get another job.

'Where is it?' he asked.

'Right aboard the ship we are loading. It will be sailing tomorrow morning for New Orleans. They are looking for a cook's helper, paying close to the same wages you are receiving here, and found in everything. I would have taken the job but I have a wife and two kids I don't want to leave,' said the foreman.

That sounded good to Phil. It meant he wouldn't have to go tramping around New York looking for a job.

'I'll go aboard with you when we get a break and see the captain. He may take you on,' the foreman said.

At 3 p.m. when the lunch break came, Phil and the foreman went aboard the ship. It was a five-masted wooden vessel with a thirty-five foot beam. The foreman went to the purser's office and asked to see the mate. In a few minutes the mate arrived wearing what looked like a military uniform. 'What can I do for you, gentleman?' he politely asked.

'I see you have a sign posted for a cook's helper, is that the case?' asked the foreman.

'Yes, we need a man to assist the cook. He doesn't necessarily have to know anything about cooking. All he has to do is work hard, do what he's told, and be able to get up whenever required,' said the mate.

'I have a man here with all those qualifications. He has been working with me and he's a hard worker but he's ready for a change. I told him about the job offered here and encouraged him to come and see you,' said the foreman.

'As cook's helper you will be peeling spuds, washing dishes, mopping floors and doing anything else the cook wants done,' said the mate as he looked over at Phil.

'I'm prepared to do all that and more,' said Phil.

'Okay, we'll give you the job. The pay is thirty cents an hour and found, and we'll supply you with work clothes.'

The mate checked everything out with the captain who advised that Phil should be aboard by ten that night. At 6:30 p.m. Phil arrived back at his boarding house and told his friends from Newfoundland he was going to work on

an ocean going vessel bound for the Caribbean. After
supper, he packed his clothes bag and headed for the ship,
the *South Sea Commander*.

CHAPTER
3

With his clothes bag slung over his shoulder, Phil walked up the companionway and attempted to go aboard the *South Sea Commander*. A guard stood near the top entrance and signaled for him to stop.

'Do you have business aboard, young man,' asked the guard.

'Yes sir, I'm going to join the ship as one of the crew. I'll be working as a second cook,' Phil replied.

The guard took a piece of paper from his coat pocket and held it close to his eyes. 'What's your name?' he asked.

'Phil Reeves.'

'Okay, you can come aboard. But before you do I have to see what you've got in your bag.'

Phil opened the bag and handed it over to him. The guard took a look and gave it back. 'Captain's orders,' he said. 'Nothing comes aboard without the mate knowing about it first.'

Phil didn't comment.

'Who do you have to report to?' asked the guard.

'The chief cook,' Phil replied.

'That must be old Jack Madison. I hope you can cook better than him, but I have to say you are very young for a cook. I'd say Jack'll have you mopping floors.'

'Suits me fine,' said Phil.

'Follow me,' said the guard as they headed towards the galley.

The *South Sea Commander* had living quarters for the ordinary sailors and galley workers below deck. The captain and first officers' quarters, including their dining room, were directly above at deck level. The captain's sleeping quarters, chart room and wheel house were above in the second story. Phil followed the guard down a fleet of stairs. He could smell food cooking as he entered the galley.

'Jack, hey Jack,' called the guard.

'Yes, boss, what do you want?' a deep voice replied.

'I have your new man here. You had better come and take charge of him or I'll give him to someone else.'

In a few minutes Jack appeared, carrying a large steaming pot.

'This is Phil...ahhh, what did you say your name was?' the guard asked as he looked at Phil.

'Phil Reeves sir,' he replied.

'This is your boss, Jack Madison, the cook,' said the guard.

Jack put down the pot and shook hands. Jack Madison wasn't concerned about the age, size or color of anyone who came to work for him. He was only interested in one thing: could that person work, was he worth his salt? Phil couldn't help staring at the cook; he had never been so close to a black man before.

'I'm Jack Madison, the one everyone hates. They don't like my cooking, yet everyone eats everything I make and comes back for more,' Jack said with a grin. 'Come on now and I'll show you to your room. You'll be in a room with one of the stewards, a young fellow like yourself.'

They walked down a narrow hallway until they came to

a door. 'The steward's name is Simon. He's an awful fellow for getting seasick, but don't mind that, you'll find him alright. After you get rid of your clothes bag come with me and I'll take you to the stores where you can get a couple of blankets.' Jack said.

After Phil had his blankets spread over the bunk and his clothes bag secured under his bunk he went to the kitchen to get the clothes he had to wear in the kitchen.

'We'll sit down and have a coffee and I'll tell you what you have to do,' Jack said. He put two mugs on the table and poured coffee. He also put out part of a molasses cake and butter and invited Phil to help himself. The two men sat in the light of a large oil lamp.

'You will start work at 6 p.m. and work till twelve midnight. You'll also work from 7 a.m. to noon. You are not to leave the ship unless I give you permission. I am to be your boss as long as you're working in this galley.'

Phil nodded in agreement.

'Your duties will be peeling vegetables and washing them, washing dishes, mopping the floors and looking after the lamps. You will begin your duties tomorrow morning at seven. I'll have someone wake you around six.'

Phil said fine and went to his room.

CHAPTER
4

The *South Sea Commander* was fully loaded with cargo for ports along the Florida coastline and points in the Caribbean. The plan was to deliver cargo around Florida and further in the Gulf of Mexico, then take on goods for Cuba and the West Indies. The ship would go on to the Barbados Islands for a part load of molasses, then come back to Cuba and finish loading with sugar for New York and further north along the eastern seaboard. The trip usually took four weeks, but this was winter and the weather could be unpredictable so it was best to figure on six weeks.

Captain Fleming briefed his officers on the details of the voyage. They had made similar voyages along the route before, but never during the winter. The captain said it wasn't the hurricane season so there wasn't much to worry about as far as storms were concerned. He ordered the officers to brief all the men and let him know if anyone had any complaints. If they had, he said, they would be dealt with before leaving port.

The *South Sea Commander* was a gallant sight as it left the port of New York. She was in fine trim with all the canvas hoisted aloft. There was not much wind blowing as the vessel moved to the southwest. Although it was January, the temperature was in the mid-teens.

Phil reported for duty at 6 a.m. His first job was taking

care of the garbage disposal. Then Jack showed him how to make toast over the hot stove and where to stack it. Jack Madison was impressed by the speed with which Phil worked. He could do more work than any three men the cook had ever had working for him. Jack noticed that Phil peeled vegetables with lightning speed. Phil had been fishing since age seven and was well used to working with knives. The cook was very impressed with him. After he had finished peeling the vegetables, Phil started washing dishes and mopping the floors. Jack didn't have to tell him twice what he wanted done. Phil quickly proved he was reliable.

The ports of call along the Florida coast were a new experience for Phil. He'd never dreamed the world could be so much different. Although it was January, it felt like summer. Phil had thought the whole world was covered in ice and snow during January, the same as it was back home in Canada Harbour. He preferred this warm weather.

After the ship delivered the cargo it had for ports around the Gulf of Mexico it still had a half load of salted cod to be delivered around the West Indies. The trip around these parts was very slow going due to the contrary winds, but the skill of the crew kept the ship going in the proper direction most of the time. Whenever the sun was shining or the stars were out the navigator was continually using the sextant and plotting the ship's location on a chart.

One afternoon, the mate informed the crew a storm was brewing. He said they were going to have a southeaster. During the night a terrible storm came on and lasted for twenty-four hours. Phil had never seen such a storm before. Neither had most of the crew aboard. The *South Sea Commander* lost part of her canvas, but she handled herself magnificently drifting with the wind. The next evening the ship was proceeding on its journey with a favorable breeze.

After the half load of salt fish was delivered, the ship sailed for Bridgetown, Barbados, in fair weather. When they arrived in port and he looked at the wharf Phil found it hard to believe there could be so many large barrels in one place, they seemed stacked as far as he could see. He asked Jack what the barrels were filled with and Jack grinned and said it was molasses, dark molasses. Phil was familiar with molasses; it was used during every meal in Canada Harbour.

'Is this where molasses is made?' he asked Jack.

Jack told him it was, and commented that a lot more "stuff" was made there too. Phil didn't know what he meant and never asked. The *South Sea Commander* took on a full load of sixty gallon barrels stamped dark molasses. The barrels were stacked in the hold and on deck; the ship was very low in the water. After the last barrel went aboard and the agent did the paperwork the captain came on board and lost no time getting underway. It was late evening and he set sail under the cover of darkness.

The heavily laden ship was soon out in the Atlantic and heading back to New York. Captain Fleming held a meeting with his officers and they all agreed to take the southern route into the Caribbean rather than go out into the Atlantic further to the northeast. The officers thought it strange Captain Fleming would go this route. They figured the open Atlantic would be the best route, especially at this time of year. But no one commented.

CHAPTER
5

After several days sailing westward, the wind seemed to die out completely. The ocean seemed motionless except for a growing swell that lazily rolled the ship. The navigator informed the captain of their exact location. They were ninety miles west-northwest of the Barbados Islands and almost directly on the equator.

At first there wasn't much attention paid to the blazing sun that came close to scorching the deck of the wooden ship. But after the third day the captain became concerned when he saw signs of paint peeling off the railing and bulges appearing in some of the barrels. Captain Fleming summoned his officers to the bridge for an emergency meeting. 'Have you examined the cargo on deck, gentlemen?' he asked.

The mate said he had and was aware several barrels were bulging due to the scorching heat from the hot sun. The captain said if the barrels burst it would not only cause a terrible mess but might result in a fire. He said that had happened on a ship a few years ago. Not one of his officers had heard of that, and they weren't worried if a few barrels of molasses burst open. As far as they were concerned, there was no threat to the ship. The captain said as a precaution, though, he wanted the sailors to pour seawater over the barrels in an effort to cool them down.

As the captain and officers were talking, the boatswain

came and said he wanted a private word with the skipper.
The boatswain said several barrels were leaking and many
more were close to bursting open. He said the heat was
causing the seams to come open. He said too he'd
discovered what was running out was rum, pure rum, not
molasses.

Captain Fleming realized he had no choice but to come
clean. 'Listen, gentleman,' he said with a sheepish grin. 'I
have a confession to make. The barrels we have aboard are
filled with rum and not molasses. I was asked to bring back
a cargo of rum by a consortium of wealthy businessmen in
New Orleans and I promise you there will be a very healthy
bonus for each one of you when we get this rum to New
Orleans or some port in that area.'

Boatswain Harry Bulger and the other officers couldn't
believe what they were hearing. Captain Fleming was
mixed up in rum running, something he'd always been
dead opposed to. But, hey, if they were going to make extra
money who cared? Harry Bulger thought for a few
moments then said, 'If this heat keeps up much longer we
could be a ticking time bomb.'

'The glass is showing hot weather for the next few
days,' broke in the navigator.

'We don't have the manpower to continue pouring
water over the barrels on deck. If we see the barrels are
beginning to burst we will have to throw them overboard
to save the ship,' said Harry.

Captain Fleming asked his officers if they had any other
suggestions. The mate suggested covering the barrels with
tarpaulins. Harry said that was possible and it was something
they could try before they started rolling the barrels
overboard. The captain said to try anything to save the cargo.

****

It was murderously hot helping the cook prepare meals for the ship's crew. Jack Madison and Phil were continually wiping sweat from their faces. Jack had observed all the sailors on board drawing seawater and pouring it over the barrels of molasses on deck. Now they were putting tarps on the cargo. Shrewd Jack didn't say much but he realized what was going on and the less said the better. Phil heard him muttering under his breath, 'I guess we're rum runners now and I only hope to God we don't get caught.'

****

After ten days with no letup from the blistering sun, Captain Fleming was becoming a very worried man. After the second week drifting with the current and watching the paint peeling from the sides of the ship, some of the men started getting sick; this included the steward who served the captain and officers. The young man came down with a high fever and couldn't get up from his bunk. Jack told Phil he would have to take on the steward's duties.

'You'll have to take the meals to the captain's dining room twice a day starting this evening,' he said as he sat Phil down and told him in no uncertain terms what was expected of him as a steward for the top brass aboard the ship.

'The captain is a very strict man, he doesn't take any foolishness from anyone. He is capable of throwing people overboard if he doesn't like them," Jack said."You will deliver the first meal at 5 p.m. so you can begin by preparing yourself. Make sure you're clean and wearing a white steward's jacket, and for the love of Mike don't spill anything. Above all, keep your mouth shut, never ask questions and don't repeat anything you hear.' Jack went on to demonstrate how to carry a fully loaded tray. He had a lot of confidence in the young Newfoundlander. If there was anyone aboard qualified for the job he knew it certainly was Phil.

CHAPTER
6

Phil entered the dining room carrying dishes and a large pot of coffee. He was expecting to see a table full of people but as luck would have it, no one was there. He set the table for six, put the coffee pot in the center of the table, and then rang a bell as Jack had instructed. Leaving the dining room, he closed the door gently behind him.

On his second trip to the dining room he was carrying a tray full of plates filled with cooked vegetables. When he opened the door he was surprised to see the captain sitting at the head of the table surrounded by his five officers. They all stared at him when he entered. Phil carefully laid the tray on a serving table and started handing out plates filled with food, beginning with the captain.

There was silence in the room until the mate said, 'Captain, this is the new steward. He's replacing Simon who has taken sick and can't get out of bed.' No one spoke. Finally the mate asked, 'What did you say your name was, Steward?'

'Phil Reeves, sir.'

The captain looked his way and nodded. Phil was about to leave when the captain asked where he was from.

'I'm from Newfoundland, sir,' Phil replied.

'From Newfoundland. Hey, we came from there just a month ago. I bet if we were close to these shores now there would be lots of wind blowing,' the captain said.

'Yes, sir. Newfoundland is where the wind was made,' Phil grinned.

'Sometimes you need it, most times you don't, this is one time we need it.' Captain Fleming seemed to be talking to the officers.

Phil went back down to get the rest of their evening meal. After the meal was served and the captain and officers had gone to their quarters, the cook told Phil to go to the dining room and collect the dirty dishes. He said to make sure the table and floors were spotlessly clean. Phil took the cleaning materials and went back up to the dining room. He collected the dirty dishes and folded the tablecloth.

As he began wiping down the table, something oddly familiar caught his eye. Hanging on the wall about four feet away from him he saw a picture he thought he had seen before. Looking at it closely, he was convinced he'd seen it somewhere before. Hearing one of the officers coming he took his eyes off the picture and went back to cleaning the dining room. He then left the dining room and returned to the galley, anxious to know what he had to do next.

'Around 9 p.m. take a pot of fresh coffee, a tray of sandwiches and some cake to the dining room for a midnight lunch. Don't forget forks, spoons and plates for everyone,' Jack told him.

The heat was stifling when Phil went back up to the dining room shortly before nine. He put his heavy tray on the table and laid plates and silverware in each place with much care. After everything was neatly in place, he turned to leave the dining room. As he did, he again found himself face to face with the painting on the wall. This time he paid more attention and looked more closely at it, but try as he might he could not remember where he had seen it before.

Phil left the dining room and went back down to the galley. After an hour of cleaning dishes, silverware, pots and pans, Phil finished his day's work mopping floors. At approximately 11 p.m. he went to his room. It was too hot to get into his bunk so he lay on top of the blanket. After a hard day's work he felt exhausted and went quickly to sleep.

****

While telling the story to Baxter Gillard many years later, Phil said he didn't know how long he had been sleeping when he fell into some kind of trance, or maybe it was a bad dream. He said it seemed as though he was being chased by something that didn't appear to be human. It seemed like something that had come up out of the water covered in seaweed.

****

'I started to run,' he said. 'I crawled into a big iron pipe, the pipe began to get smaller and I had to get on my hands and knees and start crawling. Finally, I had to get on my stomach to try to get through the pipe, then I got stuck. I could see the end not far away, but I couldn't get any further. As I lay there I saw something in the distance not far outside the pipe. I stared at it and saw it was the picture I had seen hanging on the wall in the dining room. It glowed so bright it hurt my eyes. Then I heard a voice calling, 'Phil, Phil, can't you recognize the picture on the wall?' I tried and tried but couldn't. I stared at the picture for some time. Finally the voice said, 'Phil, don't you recognize my voice?' and at that moment I did. It was Mom calling me as plain as day. I said, 'Yes Mom, it's you. I'm here stuck in this iron pipe and it looks like this is where I will die.'

'You won't die if you can identify the picture on the wall. Look at it again,' she urged me. I looked at the picture closely but couldn't tell her what it was. Then I asked her to tell me what it was. 'Don't you remember there's an identical picture in your Grandmother Carroll's house in Conche?' she said. 'It's a picture of the Harbour Grace Affray.'

I recalled it then and replied, 'Yes, I remember now. But what has that got to do with me? Why am I stuck in this iron pipe? I had nothing to do with the Harbour Grace Affray.'

She replied, 'But now you have to play a big part in breaking the spell that your ship is caught in. Can't you remember the story your Grandmother Carroll told you?'

Phil instantly remembered the whole story and knew immediately that the picture he had seen hanging on the wall in the captain's dining room was the same as the one hanging in Conche.

He awoke bathed in sweat and leaped out of bed. For a few minutes he didn't know where he was. He sat on the edge of the bunk as his senses slowly came back.

****

Jack Madison heard all the commotion in Phil's room and knew something wasn't right. He opened the door and peeked inside. 'What's the matter in there?' he asked.

'Cook, I just had a nightmare,' said Phil as he stepped out into the hallway. He knew there was something he had to do.

'I would say you did, young man. You were screaming at the top of your lungs. I hope you're not getting sick like the rest of the men. If you are, I'm in deep trouble.'

'I have to talk to you, Jack,' said Phil.

'Come sit down and we'll have a coffee,' said Jack.

Phil told Jack about his dream. He also told him the story of the picture. He said his grandmother had told him how on Boxing Day in 1883 Catholics and Protestants had clashed in Harbour Grace, Newfoundland, in an incident known as the Harbour Grace Affray. The result was five men killed and seventeen wounded. As well, 27 men were arrested.

One of those killed was a Catholic man named Patrick Callahan and somehow Phil's father Pat got most of the blame for his death.

Afterwards, an old lady who was a relative of Patrick Callahan's got someone to paint a picture of the Harbour Grace Affray and she put a curse on it.

The old lady said if the picture was ever hung on a ship's wall disaster would follow and the only way to break the spell was to take the picture down, turn it backwards, and draw a picture of the ship on the back. On land, the situation was reversed; if the drawing of the ship was displayed the curse would follow.

Believing there was just one copy of the painting and hoping no one would ever be affected by the curse, Pat stole it and brought it with him to Canada Harbour. Years later, Grandmother Carroll took the picture to Conche and hung it in her front room.

****

Jack said if Phil told Captain Fleming the story of the picture he might think he was some kind of witch and have him thrown overboard. Jack looked worried but he said they had to tell the captain. He said the heat and calm now affecting the ship was probably due to the curse.

The cook thought for a few moments. 'I'm going to

send word to the mate to come here and you can tell him
the whole story like you told me,' he said.

'Okay,' said Phil. 'We'll do it tomorrow afternoon.'

'No, we'll do it now. I'll send someone and tell him to
come here right away,' said Jack.

It took only a few minutes for the mate to arrive. He
was on duty and not in a pleasant mood. Phil looked at the
clock on the wall and saw it was past midnight. The ship
was still stifling hot.

'What do you want me for at this hour of the night,
Jack? Are you coming down with the heat sickness?' the
mate bellowed.

'No, we want to talk to you for a few minutes about a
certain matter,' said Jack, noting that the mate seemed
relieved to hear they were not sick. 'Sit to the table and
have a coffee while we tell you something. It's a matter that
concerns the steward here.'

'What's the trouble with him?' the mate asked.

'No trouble at all,' Jack said.

'Well, what's wrong?'

'Phil comes from Newfoundland and he figures there's
something aboard this ship that has put a curse on her,' Jack
said in a very shaky voice.

The mate stared at Phil with eyes blazing. 'What in
God's name are you talking about?' he bellowed.

'Tell him, Phil, what you told me,' said the cook.

'Yes s-s-sir,' stammered a scared looking Phil.

'Yes sir, what?' the mate asked.

'The picture on the wall in the captain's dining room,
sir. I've seen it before, it's a picture of the Harbour Grace
Affray. It should never be hung aboard a ship. Back home
they say if it's hung on the wall aboard a ship a curse is
guaranteed to fall on it,' said Phil.

The mate put his hand to his forehead and wiped away sweat. 'Wait till the skipper hears this, he'll go insane,' he said.

The three men were silent as they stared at each other. Then the mate jumped up and grabbed his hat. 'I'm going for Captain Fleming right now. You two stay here and talk to no one. And Phil, you'd better have your story straight because Captain Fleming will want to see you immediately. This is serious.'

Phil was nervous but he knew he would have to face Captain Fleming and explain about the curse.

'Phil, you're a good young fellow and a hard worker. You haven't given me any problems since you came aboard, but I think this is one time you've got yourself in a whole lot of trouble.' Jack paused for a few moments then added, 'Let me warn you. If you can't convince Captain Fleming that the picture on his wall has something to do with this mess we're in, then you could be swimming with the fishes before daylight.'

'I'll explain it to him just as I know it. And then, come hell or high water, if I have to swim, I'll swim, but I won't be the only one.' Phil was angry now, not frightened. All he was trying to do was help.

The mate had not been gone long when a sailor came and informed Phil and Jack that Captain Fleming wanted to see both of them in his dining room right away. As they entered the dining room, they saw the captain and his officers sitting at the table staring at the picture on the wall. Captain Fleming turned and stared directly into Phil's face.

'What's this foolishness I've heard from the mate that a curse has been put on this ship and it's connected with that picture hanging on the wall? You had better have a good explanation. Tell us about it as quickly as you can.' The captain spoke in a tone of voice that Phil had never heard before. 'Come closer to the table,' he ordered.

Phil stepped closer; by now his legs were shaking. 'Yes sir, Captain, I'll tell you all I know about it,' he stammered.

'You'd better have a good explanation. If not, you won't be on this ship for long,' the captain said.

Phil was about to speak when the captain held up his hand. 'Now relax son, and start from the beginning,' he said. 'When did you first see that picture hanging on the wall?' Captain Fleming was trying to be as calm as possible in order to get the information he needed.

Phil again cleared his throat and began, 'When I came in here this morning to serve breakfast, sir.'

'Did you recognize the picture then?'

'No sir. When I came back with the evening meal I saw it again. I knew I had seen the picture somewhere before but I couldn't place it,' Phil said.

'So, what happened for you to have changed your mind and remember it now?'

Jack Madison held up his hand to get the captain's attention. 'Mr. Captain sir,' he said.

Fleming glanced at the cook, then shifted his stare as the mate spoke up, 'Captain Fleming," he said, 'maybe the cook can answer the question from what he told me.'

Captain Fleming looked at Jack and bellowed, 'What part are you playing in this, Jack?'

'No part sir. But we heard it all, Mr. Captain.'

'You tell me what you heard, Jack, before this sidewinder tells his version,' said Fleming.

'Well, sir, I heard Phil in his sleep calling to his mudda, he was kickin and screamin about the picture, sir. Then he started saying, 'I'll tell him, Mama, I'll tell them about it, I'll tell them why, I'll tell them all about it' then he awoke in a bed of sweat.'

For a moment Captain Fleming didn't know what to say, but he thought there must be something to this. 'Listen,' he said, 'When I was in St. John's about six weeks ago I bought that picture in a pawn shop, paid five dollars for it and thought I got a good bargain. Before I left Bridgetown I remembered I had it aboard and hung it on the wall. It looked okay to me, and still does.'

The mate looked at Phil. 'Tell us more about the picture,' he said.

'Yes, continue,' said Fleming, also looking at Phil.

'When I was growing up in Canada Harbour, I used to hear my father and some of the old people talking about the picture of the Harbour Grace Affray. It was always said that as long as it hung on a wall in a building on land it was okay. But, if it was ever hung on a wall aboard a ship or anywhere over the water bad luck was sure to follow. I think what's happening on the ship now might be caused by that picture. There could be a spell on the ship,' said Phil.

The captain was furious. He had never heard the likes of this in all his thirty years of sailing. A spell cast on his ship indeed! He turned to the mate and said, 'There's only one way to see if there's anything to this. Take that damn picture down and heave it overboard.'

Phil held up his hand. 'No, no captain, you can't do it that way,' he said.

"What are you talking about?" Fleming asked.

'They say if something like this happens aboard a ship or schooner, in order to break the spell, someone has to turn the picture over and draw a sketch of the vessel on the back. Then it has to be hung back on the wall in the same place,' said Phil.

That made Captain Fleming even more furious. He turned to Phil and roared, 'Are you a witch? Do you have a

Black Art Book aboard this vessel with you?'

Phil hardly knew how to answer. 'No sir. Captain, I am not a witch and I don't have anything with me only my work clothes. Maybe I should never have opened my mouth about that picture, but I thought I should let someone know about what was always said back in Newfoundland.'

'Maybe we should do what he says,' said the mate. 'Get someone to sketch the ship on the back of the picture and hang it back on the wall and see if the wind comes on and the cursed heat gives way.'

'Okay mate, get at it right away. Take that picture apart and draw a picture of this ship on the back side. Have it completed and hung on the wall again before the sun comes up,' said a very angry Captain Fleming. He stabbed Phil in the chest with his forefinger and ordered, 'You draw the picture of this ship, you and the mate, and have it hanging on the wall before sunup. If not, you and the mate and the picture will be going overboard, out over the side and into that stinking ocean.'

Captain Fleming turned and dashed to his room, leaving the mate, Jack, and Phil reaching out for the picture of the Harbour Grace Affray.

CHAPTER
7

It was a long night for Jack, Phil, the mate and especially for the navigator who got involved with frantically trying to sketch the image of the *South Sea Commander* on the back of the picture using a and a ruler.

****

Captain Fleming awoke early and listened for sounds that usually came from an active ship, but there were none. He thought about the goings on concerning the picture and what Phil had told him. He wondered was it possible the young steward was some kind of wizard who had cast a spell on him and his ship. 'Ah, that couldn't be,' he said out loud. 'I don't believe in the likes of that.'

He thought more about the picture. The steward hadn't been there when he bought it. Things only started going wrong after he had put it up on the wall when he was leaving Bridgetown. Maybe a curse was falling on him because he was smuggling rum, maybe it wasn't the picture at all. Captain Fleming sat up and put his head in his hands. He was still wearing his clothes. He hadn't taken them off before his three hours of sleep. He glanced through the porthole at the early dawning. The sky was blazing red. He rubbed his eyes and looked again. 'I don't believe it,' he said out loud. He went out and opened the door to the dining room. He saw the mate and the navigator sitting at the table. 'Hey, listen,' he shouted.

The two men looked at him but never spoke, however the look on their faces was enough to say, 'Yes, we know.'

Fleming stared in the direction of the picture and immediately saw the sketch of his ship plainly displayed there. He walked closer and examined it further, 'You did a good job, men,' he said.

No one commented.

'Have you seen the dawning?' he asked.

'We have seen it,' they said together.

The navigator spoke up. 'Red sky in the morning, sailors take warning. It's going to blow, captain,' he said with a grin.

'You two men go to bed. You deserve a few hours sleep,' Captain Fleming turned to go to his room then stopped and said, 'Mate, tell the steward I want to talk to him around noon.'

Around ten that morning the wind started to pick up from the east and rain began to fall.

The *South Sea Commander* got under full sail as Jack Madison was standing near the stove attending to a pot of vegetables. 'I could shout alleluia this morning, Phil,' he yelled.

'I could say worse than that, Jack. Because before it's all over if they throw that picture overboard we could end up on the rocks somewhere.'

'What do you mean by that?' Jack asked.

'The picture has to be left on the wall until we get into port. Only then can it be taken down,' said Phil. 'We'll tell the mate when I bring up breakfast.'

The cook was worried, he didn't want to leave it too late. But in just a few minutes the mate came into the galley to tell Phil that Captain Fleming wanted to talk to him around noon. He said too the sky was beginning to cloud over.

'Phil's got something more to tell ya, sir,' said Jack.

The mate looked at Phil and asked, 'Yes, what is it?'

'Don't throw that picture overboard, sir. The old people used to say if you tossed it overboard before your voyage is finished the ship will go ashore on the rocks.'

The tired mate sat at the table. He put his face into his hands and cursed as he realized he would have to make another trip to see the captain.

****

Captain Fleming refused to be in the dining room as long as the drawing of his ship hung on the wall. He sat in his office and asked Phil to tell him all about the picture. After he'd heard the whole story he could understand why a curse accompanied the picture. Phil told him he would be leaving the ship when they went into port and said he would take the picture with him. The captain was happy to know that.

As it happened, the *South Sea Commander* didn't go into the port of New Orleans. It anchored off shore and company agents came out in a pilot boat to take the rum some other place for unloading. The captain very quietly told Phil to take the picture off the wall and prepare himself to disembark from his ship. He said the purser would pay him what he was owed for the voyage. Phil had his duffel bag already packed. He went to the captain's dining room and took the picture from the wall. He removed the clips that held the frame in place then rolled the picture up and put it into his duffel bag. With that done, he walked to the purser's office and collected his pay. The purser said the captain had ordered he be given an extra month's pay. Phil shook hands with Jack Madison who said he would never forget him. The two never met again.

****

Doctor Gillard asked me if I would like another cup of strong tea. He said I'd only heard part of the story and the most interesting part was just coming up if I had the time to listen.

"If someone didn't want to hear the rest of this story, then they shouldn't be asking questions," I said.

Doctor Gillard poured his tea, sweetened it, and continued the tale.

****

Phil left the ship and was glad to put his feet on the cobblestones of New Orleans. He'd had an experience he would never forget. It was a story he told a thousand times, but no one would believe him.

Phil had money in his pocket, enough to pay his passage home. However, it was wintertime and all boats had stopped running north. He had no choice but to get a place to stay and a job while waiting for spring to roll around. He went to the warehouses on the docks and landed a job with a company shipping fresh fruit to ports overseas. He said in later years it was the best job he had in all his life. Phil worked there for a year before deciding to head home to Canada Harbour. He got on a boat going to New York and Boston and worked there for a couple of months before joining a vessel going to St. John's. From there, he got on the mail steamer heading north to Canada Harbour.

****

"Before I go further into telling this story," said Dr. Gillard, "I should tell you a little about John Reeves Jr. the merchant. He was a first cousin of Phil. His father was John Reeves Sr. the older brother of Phil's father, Patrick. John came to Canada Harbour before Patrick arrived, running from the law. John Sr. was a very successful trap fisherman, but his son John Jr. had a yen to be in business from the time he was a boy. Young John was a born entrepreneur. When he was a young fellow, it was said he made more money selling cod tongues and fish fins from the scraps people threw out than was made from fish that was salted and dried. When he was just a very young man, John Jr. fell in love with Mary-Ellen Stuckless and married her. His father wasn't happy about the union because Mary-Ellen was the sister of the fish merchant Joe Stuckless whom they all hated, but he kept his mouth shut and said nothing.

"John quickly took over the business from his brother-in-law and wanted to expand it, but Joe wasn't interested in expanding. However, when Joe died at age fifty-four, Mary-Ellen, his only relative, and her husband John Reeves Jr., became the sole owners of the fish buying business and John seized the opportunity to immediately start expanding. He formed a company called John Reeves Ltd. which soon became a leading buyer of fish products on the Northern Peninsula of Newfoundland. Headquarters were in Englee, five miles across Canada Bay from Canada Harbour. John expanded into the lumbering industry and exported wood to the United Kingdom and other European countries. He got into the canning business, the boat building business and he established a cooperage industry. He also became one of the leading frozen fish businessmen in Newfoundland. At the age of seventeen, I, Baxter Gillard, became one of his managers and stayed with the company for sixty years. Earl, I'm the only one living, as far as I know, that can tell you the story about Phil Reeves, so listen carefully."

****

Phil was gone from home for six years. He didn't contact his family in Canada Harbour during that time, but his Uncle Leo kept them informed whenever Phil visited him in St. John's.

Phil's family was very happy when he finally returned home. It was reported he had a lot of money and some said it was from rum running, but no one knew for sure. Phil was welcomed home by his family with open arms. He had gifts for everyone. His mother unpacked his luggage and handed out the gifts; it was Christmas in June. As she handed out the gifts she came across a rolled up scroll secured in brown wrapping paper and marked "chart." She laid it to one side and proceeded to unpack his clothes. She put the rolled up chart on the partition over the bed.

One night after Phil had a few drinks of moonshine he began telling his father and some of his friends about the picture on the wall incident on the South Sea Commander. He said the captain had put the blame on him and said he was a wizard and he came close to being thrown overboard.

His family didn't believe him. His father said there were only a few pictures like that made and each one had a number on it. He said 'You had to be involved in the racket in order to get one of them pictures, so I can guarantee you there wasn't a picture on board some foreign going ship down in the West Indies smuggling rum.'

'This is one time you're wrong, Dad, because I have the picture. I brought it home with me, got it in my clothes bag,' Phil said.

His father said he wanted to see it so Phil went to his clothes bag but found it empty. He asked his mother what she had done with the picture. 'I never saw any picture in the bag, I took out all your stuff, there was no picture there,' she told him.

Phil couldn't believe it. He was sure he had put the picture in his clothes bag, but he had not told his mother it was rolled up in brown paper and marked "chart."

Phil Reeves was always accused of making up the story regarding the incident in the Caribbean. It was only a tall tale as far as the old timers were concerned.

It is not known how long the rolled up picture lay above the ceiling of Patrick Reeves' house, however John Reeves later bought the property to make room for business expansion.

While the men were beating down the house they discovered the rolled up picture. They never bothered to unroll it, thinking it was an old chart. They immediately turned it over to John Reeves who took it to his home in Englee without examining it.

Again, the rolled up picture was left on a shelf in the Reeves home, in a dark closet among some old charts.

CHAPTER
8

John Reeves was a very busy man. Most of his life he put in sixteen-hour workdays, so he wasn't interested in looking at old charts. Some say he had very little school education, that he found it difficult to sign his name, but he was a business genius. As the years rolled on, John Reeves Ltd. became a giant enterprise. John could not keep up with the paperwork; he had to hire accountants and managers to keep his various enterprises running smoothly.

At the age of forty, he and Mary-Ellen were very wealthy. When they were fifty, they semi-retired and were seldom seen around the business. Now, John had lots of time on his hands to browse around the mountains of old junk he had collected and stored in different places around his property. One day, while rooting through old trash under his stairs, he came across a rolled up chart. He'd had dozens of schooners and large vessels over the years so it wasn't unusual for him to see charts stacked around. He took the chart to his study and unrolled it. To his surprise he found out it wasn't a chart at all. 'Now then,' he said, 'What have we got here? It's some kind of picture.'

****

"John examined it," said Dr. Gillard. "I can see him now, adjusting his steel rimmed glasses and studying the wording. But because he couldn't read he called for me to come to his house." Dr. Gillard took a drink of tea and continued. "I wasn't concerned about being called to his house because he always wanted to discuss something, especially about the salt fish we were buying. But when I walked into his office and saw the picture spread out on the table it attracted my attention. 'Bax,' he said, 'take a look at this, did you ever see it before?' I examined it closer, then I read the writing at the bottom for him. It said 'Harbour Grace Affray.'

"John Reeves wasn't a man to cuss, however just then he struck the table with his fist and said, 'Damn it, Bax, they always called Phil Reeves a liar when he told the story about the ship down around the Barbados that had the picture of the Harbour Grace Affray hanging on the wall, and how the picture put a curse on the ship. He always said he brought the picture home and someone stole it.'

"I said to him, 'This may not be the picture, there could be dozens of them around like this,' but he said 'No, there was only one more picture like this on the whole coast and that was owned by Grandmother Carroll in Conche. Pat Reeves gave it to her. You had to be involved in the Harbour Grace Affray to own one.'

"John said he could prove the picture was not the one Grandmother Carroll owned. I asked him how. He looked at me over his glasses and said to turn the picture over. I turned it over and saw a five-masted ship drawn on the back. John said 'Look at the name that's drawn on the ship and tell me what it is.' I looked closer and said *South Sea Commander.* 'That's it," he said. 'I've heard Phil tell the story a thousand times about when he sailed on the *South Sea Commander.*'

"Then I asked him, 'John, how did you come in

possession of this picture?' He thought for a few seconds then replied, 'I know how I got it. I bought the Reeves's old house and had some men tear it down. I told them to save anything that was of any value. Someone thought this was a chart and gave it to me and I put it under the stairs with the other junk.' I asked what he was going to do with it now. He said Phil was coming to visit soon and he would get him to tell the story about what happened. He said he was going to try and buy the picture from Phil or else he could take it."

Dr. Gillard took a breath and went on with the story.

****

A week or so afterwards, Phil Reeves came to Englee. I told him John wanted to see him so the two of us went over to his house. John showed Phil the picture and explained how he got it. Phil was very shook up when he saw the picture and it took him a while to regain himself. John poured him a drink of rum and asked him to tell us the whole story that he had told so many times, which he did. When he was finished he was in tears and on his fourth drink.

'I want to buy the picture from you, Phil,' said John.

'I can't sell you something I never owned,' he replied. 'You can keep it.'

****

"Earl," Dr. Gillard said to me, "John Reeves gave Phil a bottle of rum and asked me to make a frame for the picture, which I did. It's the same frame that you're looking at now."

I felt a little restless and I guess he sensed it, because he asked me if I wanted to hear the rest of the story.

"Yes, I have the time if you do," I said.

"Okay, pour another cup of tea," he said and continued to talk.

****

One morning not long after I had been called to discuss the picture with John Reeves, I was sitting in my upstairs office in the salt fish building when someone rushed in and told me John had committed suicide.

'Good God, do you know what you're talking about?' I asked.

He said he did. Everyone in the store had heard the rifle shot and two men from Canada Harbour went to John's house and discovered him with the top blown off his head. It was something for us to face and I knew I would have to take the leading role in doing whatever had to be done. I walked over to the store and talked to Bernard MacDonald. He said a fellow named Nix Hynes and another chap went to the house when they heard Mary-Ellen screaming and discovered it all.

Bernard said he didn't have the nerve to go to the house, so I got Martin Barnes and off we went. We found John on the floor in his office, the same place where he and I had looked at the picture of the Harbour Grace Affray a few days before. It was a hard sight.

I said we would have to send for the priest in Conche and the police in St. Anthony. I found the key to his office and proceeded to close the door and lock it, but when I was closing the door I saw something that caught my eye. I opened the door again. Sure enough, the picture of the ship hung on the wall. It was the same one you're looking at now. I thought about what Phil Reeves had said about how bad luck would follow if a drawing of a ship with the picture of the Harbour Grace Affray on the back was hung in a building on land. I didn't say anything as I closed the door and locked it.

****

I did not comment for fear of what Dr. Gillard might think but I had to ask how he got the picture now hanging on the wall in front of me. "Just a minute," he said "I'm not finished with the story."

****

After the death of John Reeves, his wife, Mary-Ellen, went to live with Jack Farewell, their accountant. No one lived in the Reeves house after that. One evening a couple of years later, in late fall, I went home after work. I wasn't there very long before someone rushed in and told me John Reeves house was on fire. I put on my coat and hurried over. Smoke was coming from the eaves; you could tell the inside was engulfed in flames. Some men went inside and started taking out whatever they could save. The house wasn't very far from the retail stores and all the company records were in the main offices upstairs. I knew there was a danger of losing the whole complex so I got a few men and went to the offices and tried to save as much of the records as possible. As it turned out, all of the businesses on this side of the harbour burned down. It was a massive fire.

In the morning, just after daylight, I went over to the area. Smoke was still seeping from the cinders. I just stood there and stared at it all. I was very upset. After all, this was a place where I had worked since I was sixteen years old and now it was all gone. As I turned to go home I saw something sticking out from a pile of snow. Curious, I stopped to examine it. I was very surprised when I discovered it was that picture you see hanging on the wall.

****

"It appears this picture has survived every time danger came near it, and it seems it always has a victim," I said.

"It only appears that way, it's a coincidence," said Dr. Gillard.

"I'm not sure, Doctor. I wouldn't have it hanging on my wall. From what I've heard about it, it could even cause a curse to come upon a town."

I asked Dr. Gillard if he was leaving to go to Victoria, British Columbia, to spend the winter with his daughter. He said yes, he was going very soon and if he didn't see me before he left he wished me a successful winter chasing poachers. I shook his hand and gave Mrs. Gillard a hug before I left.

During that winter I received a phone call from the lady who took care of Dr. Gillard's property, advising me that he had developed a severe case of Alzheimer's disease. In early May he returned home to Englee. I went to visit him and was surprised to find he didn't recognize me. As I talked to him in his kitchen, I again came face to face with the picture of the *South Sea Commander* hanging on the wall. Dr. Gillard passed away shortly afterwards, followed by his dear wife. The next year, one of their daughters came and lived in the house for a while before returning home to Surrey, B.C. because she missed her friends. Shortly after she returned to Surrey, I received news that she had suddenly passed away.

The house has not been lived in since but I suppose the picture still hangs on the wall in Dr. Gillard's kitchen, waiting for its next victim. Will it be a person, place or thing?

Herb Keefe

The temperature was -30 with high winds on the morning of January 29, 1947. Two men sawing lumber with a push-bench were working hard and although it was severely cold they were exhaling hot steam from their lungs. As the men sawed each log they had to hold it in place to make the proper cut. There was no second chance at lining it up, it had to be done right the first time.

On this cold day in January, when this particular log struck the saw, the teeth hungrily grabbed the wood as the governor on the 40-horsepower Calvin engine opened up, giving the thirty-six-inch saw more power and making it run faster.

The man at the front end of the push-bench moved quickly with the log, passing the saw along in a shower of sawdust. And then, as he should, he suddenly applied his weight to the bench and gave it a hard pull.

Herb Keefe, the man working at the rear end of the push-bench, was holding the log and pushing when he suddenly slipped on the ice covering the loose sawdust.

Herb lost his balance and stumbled forward. For a second, it appeared as if he would fall face down on the fast moving saw. But as quick as a flash Herb reached out for the log with both hands in order to protect his face. The log was almost sawed through when Herb reached out and it was too late. It was way too late.

The saw's hungry teeth grabbed the wool mitten on Herb's left hand. It took just a split second for those steel-tipped teeth to shatter the hopes and dreams of the 29-year-old logger.

Herb quickly jumped back from the bench. With a sick feeling in his stomach he looked down at his hand and his face went pale as he saw that his mitten was in shreds.

The man who was doing the sawing didn't realize what had happened until he saw pieces of the wool mitten on the bench and spouts of blood. Then he loudly screamed, "Herb has his hand sawn."

Herb somehow managed to got his mitt off. His thumb was gone, the next three fingers were severed at the knuckle. Only half the little finger was left.

"With each pump of the heart, blood was spouting in streams from the finger stumps like strings of drooping lines," Ludwick (Lud) Reid said in telling the story.

Mr. William Reid (Uncle Will), the owner of the sawmill, was a few feet away when the accident occurred. He was at the scene in seconds. "Oh no. Oh no. Herb, what in the world happened? Are you all right?" he shouted.

"My hand is gone. I'm finished, Uncle Will." Herb was white and his voice was shaking.

Uncle Will quickly grabbed Herb's wrist and applied pressure to his arm with vise-like fingers. There was no first aid equipment in the mill or anywhere else for that matter.

Lud's mother lived nearby in a log cabin and Uncle Will told him to quickly run there and get something to wrap around Herb's hand. Lud ran off as fast as he could.

"Herb has his hand sawed off. I have to get something to wrap it up in," Lud shouted as he dashed wildly into the cabin, almost knocking his mother down.

His mother immediately pulled a flannel sheet off the

bed and handed it to him. Right away, Lud was out the door and headed back to the mill. Halfway there, he met his father and three other men, all going in the same direction. When they arrived at the mill, Lud handed his father the sheet. Another man tore off a piece of material and quickly wrapped it around Herb's severed hand.

"Get the dogs ready," Uncle Will said to Lud as they helped Herb walk to the cabin. Poor Herb was so shaken he could barely walk.

Lud ran to the dog house. The Reids had eight sled dogs of the mongrel type used for hauling logs. Lud harnessed the dogs and hooked them to the komatik. He got the riding box ready and strapped it on. Back in the cabin, Lud's father was still gripping Herb's wrist, while his mother examined the hand and applied pressure to the wound. Lud could see parts of bone protruding from the severed fingers. He knew Herb Keefe was heading for a hard time.

The little town of Bide Arm, where midwife Emma Fillier (Aunt Eamy), lived was less than a mile away. Lud heard his mother say, "We'll take him to Aunt Eamy."

"No, we're going to have to take him to St. Anthony," Uncle Will spoke up right away. "Lud, you and Ches go for Roddickton as fast as you can with Herb. Ches will sit behind him and hold him. We'll harness another team and follow you."

Ches Cassell was a burly man, as strong as an ox. "Okay, Uncle Will, we'll leave immediately," he said.

Herb was led to the komatik box and seated in Ches's lap. The bleeding had stopped by now but he was in a lot of pain. The eight dogs went crazy as they ran on the trail leading to Roddickton.

****

Nurse Poplyn was from England and very staunch in her ways. She was in her clinic with a patient when she heard dogs barking and the hissing of Jumbo, her tomcat. When she heard the commotion she looked up and wasn't pleased to see the clinic door open without a knock or any warning of entry. Lud walked in.

"We have a man who has his hand sawed," he said quickly.

"Good Lord," she said. "Bring him in."

Few people burst into Nurse Poplyn's clinic without knocking; she was a woman who believed in protocol and she ruled with an iron fist. However when she saw the look of terror on Lud's face, she knew something extraordinary had happened.

"Bring the man in for God's sake," she ordered.

Ches led Herb in. The bedsheet was wrapped around his hand and arm. Nurse Poplyn was very capable even though on times she could be unpleasant and sharp.

"Sit him down here," she ordered.

Ches said he felt as though he was the one who had sawn off Herb's hand by the way she addressed him. Herb was placed in the chair with his hand on his lap.

"You have a bedsheet around his hand," Nurse Poplyn said sarcastically. "What is the extent of the wound?"

"He has his fingers sawed off," answered Lud.

She went to a cabinet and took out a bottle. Picking up a needle, she filled a syringe. "This is morphine for the pain," she said. Undoing Herb's belt buckle she pulled his pants down at the back and plunged the needle in. Herb groaned. She looked at Ches and said, "Get out." Ches bolted for the door; he said he was glad to get away from the old bat.

Nurse Poplyn carefully removed the bedsheet from Herb's hand.

"Oh my, whoever bandaged this did a superb job," she said.

Lud was silent; he didn't know if he should comment or not.

The nurse applied pressure to Herb's wounds then bandaged the hand tightly.

"How is the weather, young man?" she asked Lud.

"Not very good, Nurse. There's a blizzard on outside," he said.

"I see," she said in her crisp English accent. "Well, we are leaving for St. Anthony immediately." She called to her maid, "Go get Tom Colbourne and tell him to come here right away."

"Yes Nurse," said the maid.

Nurse Poplyn turned to Lud. "You get out and start getting the coach-box ready," she said.

Lud went out the door, happy to get out of her dispensary.

****

Tom Colborne assisted the nurse in all emergencies, especially if she had to travel the sixty miles to St. Anthony by dog-team. Tom made sure the coach-box was ready and the patient had warm blankets for traveling. It only took a few minutes for Tom to appear on the scene. He was wearing neither cap nor coat.

"Good Lord," he said when he saw Herb. Then he turned to the nurse. "I have the coach-box all ready, Nurse. It's fully equipped. All that has to be done is hook the dogs to it."

"You fellows do that right away," she said curtly.

Tom turned to Lud and Ches, who were standing just outside the door. "Okay boys," he said, "transfer the dogs to the coach-box komatik. I'll take care of your komatik."

Nurse Poplyn ordered the men to put Herb into the coach-box, where they wrapped him in heavy blankets. She came outside fully dressed in her winter clothes, ready for the dog-team trip. She carried her medical bag and a small pack-sack. "I'm ready to go when you are," she said, as if she had been waiting for hours.

"Well then, let's go," said Lud, giving her as hard a stare as he dared. "Nurse, you have to get in the coach-box, I'm ready to leave."

"I'm not getting in the coach-box, I'm standing on behind," she said.

Ches was just going to tell her she had to get into the coach-box because he was going to stand behind and help drive the dogs when they saw another dog-team pull into the yard.

It was Arthur (Art) Compton of Bide Arm who had a sawmill not far from Will Reid's. Someone had told him Herb had sawed himself badly and he came immediately to Roddickton to assist with the trip. Lud was happy Art was going with them as he was very experienced in taking patients to St. Anthony by dog-team.

With the extra dog-team on the scene, and to avoid a quarrel between the nurse and Ches (because Ches had no intention of getting in a coach-box with Herb), Lud told Ches he could return to the sawmill as they wouldn't need him. Ches was more than pleased to get away from the company of the English nurse.

****

Canada Bay is a long arm that reaches seventeen miles inland from the Labrador Sea. The towering Cloud Mountains are on the western side of the bay. The winds

that sweep down off these rugged barrens during the winter
have no pity on anyone. The wind on this particular
afternoon was northwest and coming off the mountains. It
lashed at the dogs, almost blowing them over. The wind
was so bad that Art and Lud could hardly stand up. The
wind blew the snow around so much that they had trouble
seeing anything along the snowy path.

Although the storm battered the two men, they stood
their ground. Lud tried to persuade Nurse Poplyn to get
into the coach-box on several occasions, but she insisted on
standing at the rear, clinging to the handles. In such a
storm, it was a fearsome afternoon trying to reach Main
Brook, thirty miles away.

Once they were off the bay and in among the heavy
timber, away from the wind, the going got a little better,
although the snow was very heavy and deep. Lud, who was
wearing snowshoes, had to help the dogs pull the komatik
while Nurse Poplyn pushed and walked behind the coach-
box. Lud wouldn't have been able to make it if Art had not
gone ahead and broke down most of the snow drifts. At
approximately four-thirty it became dark; the wind got
much stronger with the setting sun.

"We are going to have hard going the rest of the way,"
said Art.

Nurse Poplyn seemed worried as they crossed Lanes
Pond. She didn't like the idea of getting lost in the dark in
such a blizzard. Holding up her hand to stop the two dog-
teams, she asked Art if he knew where he was going.

"Nurse, I can smell my way along this trail with my
eyes closed. I'll tell you what, you get in the coach-box
with Herb and coverup. We'll take you out when we get to
the logging camp," said Art, who was no fool. Art had
made dozens of trips with patients along this trail to St.

Anthony, during the day and at night.

The nurse from England didn't appreciate being insulted by a Newfoundland logger. She swore under her breath and told them to move on. Several times along the way they had to stop to let the nurse attend to Herb. He was having much pain and losing blood.

Twenty-two miles into their journey, they arrived at a Bowater logging camp. It was 6 p.m. The people at the camp were expecting them. Someone at the telegraph office in Roddickton had telephoned (the old crank telephone was then in use) to inform them about Herb's accident and to leave a message for Art. His wife had taken seriously ill and he was to return home immediately. Art told Nurse Poplyn he was returning to Bide Arm right away to see what was happening back home.

The men at the camp brought Herb indoors. He was in terrible condition, losing blood and experiencing a lot of pain. He was in so much pain that tears were streaming down his face. The nurse gave him another shot of morphine and tightened the bandages around his hand.

"We have to move on," she told Lud. "We have to get to St. Anthony."

"Don't worry, Nurse, we're leaving as soon as we have a cup of tea," said Lud.

"Are you sure you know the way to Main Brook?" she asked.

"If I don't, you will be the first one to freeze to death," said Lud. The nurse didn't comment.

After they had a lunch, Herb was put back into the coach-box. It was 6:30 and very dark when Lud hauled on his snowshoes and pulled out from Camp 5, heading for Main Brook, eight miles away. Art bid them goodbye as he left for Bide Arm. The blizzard was still raging.

The journey to Main Brook was terrible even though the dogs were trained to stay on the trail and follow it. The nurse, holding to the rear of the coach-box, was almost invisible in the drifting snow and darkness. Many times along the way Lud stopped and checked to see if she was still there. He found her grimly clinging to the rear of the coach-box for dear life.

At midnight, the weary dog-team arrived at Main Brook and went to the home of Mrs. Simms, the midwife, who had received word from the Bowater office that they were on their way with a patient. Mrs. Simms helped Nurse Poplyn with the dressings on Herb's hand. Ron Ollerhead, a neighbour, had food prepared and ready for the dog-team. After the dogs had eaten, he put them in his shed to keep them from running loose.

****

Two well known men lived in Main Brook: Mr. Adolphus Rice (Uncle Doffie) and Mr. Durdle Ricks (Der Rix), a World War II veteran. These two men devoted their lives to transporting people to the hospital in St. Anthony in all kinds of emergencies and all kinds of storms; they were well known around Northern Newfoundland. Because of the blizzard, it was thought necessary to get in touch with them in this particular case.

During the night, the midwife stayed up with Herb and kept watch. He didn't sleep at all. Sometime around 3 a.m. he complained about severe pain in his hand. He also said he had a terrible pain under his arm and in his jaw. Nurse Poplyn was called. She discussed the problem with Mrs. Simms and they agreed it was a sure sign of tetanus (lock-jaw). The nurse decided to administer a shot of antitoxin. She also gave Herb another shot of morphine.

Lud told the nurse he was leaving at 6 a.m. and she promised she would be ready. At 5:30, Der Rex and Uncle Doffie arrived with a team of twelve dogs. Lud was waiting, ready to go.

"This is one of the worst blizzards I've seen in many years. It's been on going now for four days and I would say there are drifts eight feet high going around the bay," said Doffie.

"We won't be able to keep close to the shoreline then. It's best we stay off aways," said Der.

Doffie agreed.

At 6 a.m. they bid Mrs Simms farewell. She wished them good luck and they were on their way. It was dark and stormy as the two teams departed from Main Brook and headed around Hare Bay.

Lud kept close behind the larger team that was making a trail through the deep snow. Nurse Poplyn stood at the rear of the coach-box and held on tight.

Going around Hare Bay, the men had to stop the dog-teams several times in order to clean the ice and snow from the dogs' eyes, and wipe between their paws.

The two dog-teams found themselves in a full scale blizzard as daylight approached. When they got halfway around Hare Bay, Der called a halt and suggested they change direction and go closer to the shoreline for fear of running into open water.

"That's a good idea because the sea may have the ice broken up," agreed Doffie.

The teams changed direction and went closer to the shoreline. It was harder going, but safer. When daylight came, they hadn't yet reached Goose Tickle Arm. But as they pushed on, Doffie noticed the wind was changing to the northeast.

"We're in for a lot of snow if this keeps up, especially in the area of Hare Island. That's where snow was made," he told Lud.

The men kept slowly pushing their way through the snowdrifts along the shoreline. There was no doubt if the two Main Brook men had not been with Lud that day he would have had to return to Main Brook.

****

Years earlier, Dr. Grenfell had traveled the same route and ran into similar storms. For that reason, he had a log cabin built at the bottom of Hare Bay. Those who came after him kept the cabin in repair. Uncle Doffie knew where this cabin was and wanted to get there for shelter because Herb needed attention and Nurse Poplyn could not attempt to care for him out in the open in this blizzard.

Doffie stopped the dog-teams in a small cove in the shelter of heavy trees; it was a cozy place.

"This is where Dr. Grenfell's cabin is. We'll get the fire going, have a thaw out, and a cup of tea," said Doffie.

This was welcome news to the English nurse as she would be able to tend to her patient. Der Rex found the cabin and after the snow was cleared away from the entrance and the fire lit, Herb was brought inside. When they took him from the coach-box he was in a terrible state: cold, shivering, wet, and crying with pain.

"I wouldn't care if it wasn't for the pain," he told them, "I think I am going to go out of my mind, I can't stand it any more. My, oh my, it's better if I died."

"You're not going to die, Herb. You'll be fine when we get to the hospital," Lud assured him.

Der Rix made tea and shared his food with everyone.

"The worst place is going along the straight shore

inside Hare Island. That's not far from here. When we get to Boiling Brooks it will be okay from there to Locks Cove. The going should be pretty good then," Doffie told them.

****

It was 2 p.m. when the group left the Grenfell cabin. When they came out on Hare Bay the drifting snow and wind struck them forcefully as the blizzard continued. Der Rix attached a line to the head dog of Lud's team. That way, Lud wouldn't get left behind.

The men begged Nurse Poplyn to get in the coach-box, but she refused. Lud wanted to tie her on, but she refused that too. It took them two hours to travel the one mile to Boiling Brooks. The three men had to tread a road in the snow to get the dogs and coach-box through. They had a head wind all the way and by the time they reached Boiling Brooks, it was beginning to get dark. If Doffie and Der had not been familiar with the trail they would probably have gone back to Grenfell's cabin for the night.

When they got to Boiling Brooks, the trail turned right and led in a southerly direction; this gave them a side wind and much better going especially across the big bogs. Although they couldn't see the trail on the bogs, the lead dog of Doffie's team knew where to go.

It was long after dark when they reached the trail leading through the heavy timber to Locks Cove. Although the snow was deep, they made better progress. It was approximately 8 p.m. when the party reached Locks Cove and the storm appeared to be worse than ever. Only God knows what they all went through during their fourteen-hour ordeal, especially Herb with his hand half sawn off, in pain and bleeding, stuffed into a coach-box for two days, not knowing if he was going to live or die.

****

Locks Cove was the home of Lot Elliott and his wife Rachel. The Elliotts had many children and an enormous house with ten bedrooms. Lot's son, George, who now lives at Main Brook, tells the story:

****

I remember the stormy night the three men and Nurse Poplyn from Roddickton came to our door. The wind was blowing a living gale with drifting snow. The storm had been on for several days.

First we heard dogs barking. Dad said. 'You know full well there's no one out on a night like this. If it is, there's something mighty wrong.' Fred, my brother, rushed to the door and sure enough when he opened it a woman fell in across the floor. She was covered in ice and snow. Mom helped her up. The woman told us she was a nurse from Roddickton.

We pulled on our boots and coats and rushed outside. The first man we met was Uncle Doffie Rice. We knew there was something seriously wrong when we saw him and the coach-box. He told Dad about the man they had aboard with his hand sawn and the serious condition he was in. Dad told them to get the injured man into the house as quickly as they could.

There was a Reid fellow with them, Lud was his name. In fact, he was a relative of ours although we had never seen him before. The other man was Der Ricks. They all started to get the injured man out of the coach-box but Dad stopped them.

'Don't take him out,' he said. 'We'll bring the coach-box

inside. Untie it from the komatik.'

Dad went inside and told Fred and I to take the kitchen table and put it outside and bring the coach-box with the patient into the outside kitchen and that's what we did. Dad then sent us with Lud Reid and Der Ricks to get food for the dogs and a place to shelter them in for the night."

Herb, by now a total wreck, was wet and shaking with the cold. He needed to relieve himself so he was taken from the coach-box and to the toilet.

Mom provided Herb with dry clothes as he was still wearing his work clothes. She also got dry clothes for Nurse Poplyn. They were a little large but dry and warm. The nurse examined Herb's hand before Mom wrapped him in blankets and put him near the stove in the kitchen on a day bed. That's where he spent the night.

Dad told Fred and me to bring the dogs' harnesses and traces inside; we hung them behind the stove in the kitchen to dry, Dad said he wasn't worried about the smell. He said we had an emergency on out hands and the smell didn't matter. After the nurse and the three men were given beds, Mom told them to try and get some rest. She stayed up all night with Herb.

****

Lud said it was a very cold night and the lumber in the Elliott's walls were making loud cracking noises. It was, he said, the sound of frost cracking, and you would have sworn the house was going to break in two. Lud continued:

****

At 5 a.m. when Mr. Elliott got out of bed the blizzard was still raging, but there was no doubt about it. Herb had to get to the hospital at St. Anthony today and nothing was

going to stop us. Herb told me he didn't sleep at all during
the night. He said the pain was getting worse. The nurse
was up when I came downstairs, I doubt if she'd slept
during the night; she told us infection was setting into
Herb's hand. We knew that meant we had to get to St.
Anthony as soon as possible.

It was after daylight when the two dog-teams left
Locks Cove. Uncle Doffie was ahead, he wore his
snowshoes all the way. The weather was so bad you
couldn't see a hand before you.

Before we left Mr. Elliott's place, he told the nurse to
get her frame in the coach-box. He said it was no place for
a woman stuck on the side like a crow. We thought she was
going to tell him where to go, but she didn't, I guess she
was afraid because he was the type nobody could push
around.

                        ****

Going over the White Hills in a blizzard is a very tricky
experience unless you know what you're doing. One wrong
turn, said Lud, and you could find yourself hundreds of
feet below in the salty ocean of Hare Bay. He went on:

                        ****

There was a telephone line going over the White Hills
that we could follow in good weather, but on a day like we
were experiencing we couldn't see from pole to pole. The
only thing we could follow was the sound of the wind
whistling through the wires. Der Rix was the one for that,
he could hear everything. He said it was like artillery shells
they used to fire over their heads at the Germans when they
were fighting over in France.

It took us until noon to get to Ireland Bight. We went

into a fellow's house there and had lunch. After that, a group of men from there tramped a road with snowshoes up over the hill for us, from there on it was pretty good.

We arrived at the hospital around three-thirty that afternoon. Dr. Curtis was waiting for us. It didn't take long for them to take Herb inside. They rushed him into the operating room and did whatever they had to do, I think they did three or four operations. They told us he was going to be okay.

Old Nurse Poplyn almost fell headlong when they helped her in. Her legs were cramped and I suppose that was the reason she wouldn't get in the coach-box in the first place, you couldn't blame her.

****

When Lud was told he could have accommodations at the hospital annex he was pleased. Doffie and Der Rix decided to go over on the other side of the harbour to stay with relatives. Before they went, Uncle Doffie said, "Lud, unhook your dogs from the coach-box. We'll haul it back as far as Main Brook for you. That will be easier on you."

"Okay, and thanks for all you did," Lud said.

"Glad to be of service, call on us anytime, whenever you're in trouble," they said, smiling as they shook hands with him and left.

Lud fed his dogs and put them in pens provided by the hospital. The next morning he didn't harness his dogs because the blizzard was still on, although it was clear overhead. The wind had shifted to the northwest, which meant it would be blowing in their face on the way back home. Nurse Poplyn came looking for him around 10 a.m.

"Why aren't you going, young man?" she asked.

"It's still very stormy outside, Nurse. To go over the

White Hills in those conditions would be almost like committing suicide."

She stared at him. "Are you afraid now that the other two men are gone?" she asked.

Lud said her words made him mad. He said he thought he was doing her a favour by waiting for the wind to die down. He said, "Nurse, get your things ready, I'm leaving in half an hour or as soon as I get the harnesses on the dogs."

"Okay, and I think it's about time," she said, and hurried off.

Lud said coming over the White Hills they were lucky they didn't get blown off and into the ocean. The nurse sat on the box with her back to the wind. The swirling snow that curled around her and Lud almost took her breath away.

Lud only got part of the way across the hills when the nurse started screaming, "Stop the dogs. Stop the dogs."

"What's wrong, Nurse, are you afraid?" Lud asked as he brought the dogs to a halt.

"I want to turn and face the wind. I can't get my breath this way," she said.

"Nurse, you'll freeze your face unless you cover it," Lud said.

"That's my business," she said, as she turned to face the piercing wind.

The wind had no pity on Nurse Poplyn. By the time they arrived at Locks Cove that evening Lud said she was in quite a state with her face partly frozen. He and Nurse Poplyn were forced to stay another night at the Elliott home. Lud told Mr. Elliott not to blame it on him. He said the nurse wouldn't listen to anything.

"I know that," Mr. Elliott said, and added with a laugh,

"She knows now she's not back in England."

The next morning it was still stormy. The wind had shifted to northeast again with thick snow and wind, but Lud and the nurse left anyway. It was late when they arrived at Main Brook. The dogs were tired and they just couldn't travel any further. Lud and Nurse Poplyn stayed with Mrs. Simms that night.

The following morning the storm continued to rage but they left for home anyway. It was different now, though. The nurse was in the coach-box and happy to be there, and Lud was glad she was there. He said she looked an awful sight with her face all blisters but she was a tough woman. They arrived at the nursing station at 6 p.m.

Nurse Poplyn asked Lud if he wanted a cup of tea. He told her he didn't have time, he had to get home. He put the coach-box in the shed and left. He arrived back at Bide Arm around midnight. As soon as he got in the house, even before he had his coat off, his father told him to go to Pearl Keefe's house and give her the news about Herb. All in all, it was quite a trip.

The Five Toms

During the mid-1950s, Sam Drover was the Member of the House of Assembly for White Bay. While in office, he traveled almost every crook and cranny of his district. However, there were a few places he wasn't required to go. In those places, they all voted for Joey anyway.

Liberal Premier Joseph Smallwood was the first premier after Newfoundland's Confederation with Canada in 1949. Sam Drover, a former Newfoundland Ranger, was originally elected as a Liberal member of the House of Assembly in 1949, the first election after Confederation. In 1955, however, Sam grew disenchanted with Smallwood's government and crossed the floor to sit as a member of the Cooperative Commonwealth Federation (CCF). It was the first time a member of that political party sat in the Newfoundland legislature.

When Joey called a provincial election, Sam had his plans made. He would use the coastal steamers to travel around and talk to passengers getting on and off at every stop. When he came to a large town with a good boarding house he would get off, book himself in, and then hire smaller local boats to take him to small settlements, especially if he thought someone there was going to vote against Joey.

The story has it that one day in August a man by the name of Thomas Randell (Uncle Tom) came from Hooping

Harbour to Roddickton in his trap skiff to deliver a load of sawed lumber he was selling to the Saunders and Howell company. While at Roddickton, he decided to go shopping before returning home later that evening. He had a pocket full of money, payment for his lumber.

He went to William F. Newhook and Sons, a business not far from the wharf where he could purchase almost anything. While at the store, Uncle Tom was introduced to a gentleman who was a stranger in appearance but had a name that was very familiar. It was MHA Sam Drover and he was there on the campaign trail, shaking hands with people. Skipper Tom Randell had often heard the name Sam Drover, but this was his first time meeting him.

Bill Newhook, the owner of the store, was quick to score a few brownie points with his old buddy Sam. He looked at Skipper Tom and asked someone who the fine looking gentleman was. He was told the man was from Hooping Harbour and had come to sell a boatload of lumber to Saunders and Howell. Bill immediately saw a chance to secure a few votes around Hooping Harbour for Sam. Uncle Tom Randell was a very mild-mannered man. He was not one bit interested in politics and was not about to get involved.

Sam Drover held out his hand and said, "I'm Sam Drover, your MHA, and you are?"

Skipper Tom looked at the government official and hesitated for a moment. Then he held out his hand and said, "I'm Tom from Hooping Harbour."

Sam said later that Tom's work-hardened hand felt like a piece of board. He said too he recognized there was something special about Skipper Tom.

"Tom," he said, "I'm coming up your way in a few days. If you don't mind maybe I could drop in and visit you."

"I sure would love to talk to you, but you would have to come late in the evening or on a blowy day, unless you visit us down on the stage. We're busy at the fish now," said Uncle Tom.

"I'll make sure to get to see you when I come up that way." Sam hesitated for a moment then said, "By the way, I'll put some literature in the mail for you, a whole bunch of the stuff. You could probably hand it around."

"Yes, that'll be grand," said Uncle Tom, not one bit interested.

Sam Drover thanked him and went back into Bill's office. In the meantime, Uncle Tom paid for the goods he had purchased and left.

Sam Drover was impressed with the gentleman he had just met and told Bill he wanted to hire his passenger boat to go to Hooping Harbour.

"The Liberals lost the vote there in the last election so I think I'm going to have to go visit them. This Tom fellow might be a good contact. Let's face it, I'm going to need all the votes I can get," he said.

Now, a few minutes after Uncle Tom left, two young fellows wanting to buy a couple of packs of Target tobacco came into Bill's store. It was obvious they were strangers. Bill Newhook, being very inquisitive, asked them where they were from.

"We're from Hooping Harbour," one of them said.

"You must be with Tom," said Bill.

"Tom who?" said the fellow doing the talking.

"I don't know, Tom somebody, he was just here, bought some stuff and left. Said his name was Tom," said Bill, taking the half burnt cigarette from his mouth.

The young fellow grinned. "There's a lot of Toms at Hooping Harbour, sir," he said. "But I've never heard of a

Tom somebody. There could be one up there but we've never heard of anybody by that name."

Bill was about to have something else to say to this young fellow who seemed a bit too cocky for his own good. But he hesitated; he didn't want Sam to lose a couple of votes because of him.

"Have you fellows ever met Sam Drover?" asked Bill.

"No, who would that be?" they asked.

"Sam Drover is your MHA, the one who represents you in the government," said Bill, thinking they were very stupid.

"No, there must be a mistake, sir, he don't represent us, we've never heard talk of him," they said.

The two young fellows looked toward the office door and saw a distinguished gentleman standing in the doorway. Sam had heard the conversation and decided to come out. The young fellow doing the talking walked over to Sam and said, "You must be Sam Drover, the one the man was just telling us about?"

"Yes," said Sam, holding out his hand, "I'm Sam Drover."

"I'm Freeman Randell and this is Harold Randell. We're both from Hooping Harbour," said Freeman, as they shook hands.

"Good to meet you both. You fellows must be with the gentleman who just left here a few minutes ago, a Mr. ah-ah. Bill, what did he say his last name was?" asked Sam.

"I don't know who it was, Tom somebody, must be a Randell," said Bill quickly.

Sam turned to Freeman. "I told him I would send him some campaign literature in the mail, would you fellows know what his last name is, and his address?" he asked.

Freeman looked Sam Drover in the eye. He sensed Sam

was fooling around with the two Hooping Harbour youths, trying to get them going and have a laugh. However, Sam was up against the wrong fellow, crafty Freeman Randell.

"Mr. Drover, it would be quite a job for you to get a letter to Tom, or Uncle Tom as you call him, unless you know what you are doing," said Freeman.

"What do you mean by that, young man?" asked Sam in a stern voice.

"Well, Mr. Drover," said Freeman, as he looked into the face of the man who had represented his hometown for years in the House of Assembly, but had never stepped foot on Hooping Harbour soil. The closest Sam Drover ever got to Hooping Harbour was viewing the little fishing village from the top deck of the coastal steamer.

"We just got here," Freeman lied. "We're on our way to work in the Bowater camps. Never saw the Tom you're talking about. What did he look like?"

Sam Drover didn't notice the smirk on Freeman's face.

"I would say he's in his forties, kind of short, raw-boned with big hands," Sam said after a moment's thought.

Freeman grinned as he winked at Bill Newhook.

"You must have been talking to Flora's Tom or Sis's Tom, that's the same fellow. Before he got married, he was known as Sis's Tom after his mother Aunt Sissy. But after he got married to Aunt Flora they changed his name to Flora's Tom, so you could have been talking to Flora's Tom or Sis's Tom," said Freeman.

The other fellow, Harold, spoke up, "Free, I don't think he was talking to Flora's Tom, it doesn't sound like him. He might have been talking to Aunt Mary's Tom."

"What does Aunt Mary's Tom look like?" Sam asked as he looked at Harold.

Freeman held up his hand. "I'll do the talking, Harold,

because I can explain it better than you," he said.

"Well Mr. Drover, Aunt Mary's Tom used to be called Job's Tom before he got married. After he got married to Aunt Mary and got out on his own they changed his name to Aunt Mary's Tom," said Freeman.

"So Freeman, what does Aunt Mary's Tom look like? Is he anything like Aunt Sis's Tom, or what is it, Aunt Flora's Tom?" asked a frustrated Sam Drover.

"Yes, it's Aunt Flora's Tom. Well, he's a pretty strapping man, something like Aunt Jessie's Tom, only he's older," said Freeman.

He stopped for a moment to let the information sink in. Then he decided to really confuse the government representative.

"On the other hand, Mr. Drover, you could have been talking to Aunt Jessie's Tom." Freeman paused for a few seconds then added, "No, I don't think it was him." He looked quickly at the MHA and asked, "Was his mouth black?"

Sam looked puzzled for a moment, then asked, "Mouth black? Why would his mouth be black?"

"Well, Aunt Jessie's Tom got a black mouth. It happened when he was young. His teeth got rotten so Big Granny pulled one of his jaw teeth and almost drove him out of his mind. He went through so much pain he never let anyone else touch another tooth in his head, not even go handy to his mouth."

Sam was speechless as he stared at Freeman.

"His teeth all rotted off tight to his gums and grew over. His mouth looked like someone who had been poked in the mouth with a poker someone used to root the stove. His mouth is as black as the coal. Behind his back we call him Black Mouth Tom. But in front of his face we call him

Aunt Jessie's Tom," said Freeman.

There was an empty wooden biscuit box near the counter. Sam walked over to it and sat down. He had not heard the likes of this before, not even in his hometown of Hodges Cove, where he thought he had heard it all. By now Bill Newhook and the rest of the customers standing around were in their glee.

"No that was not the Tom," said Sam. "His mouth wasn't black."

Harold, the other young fellow, sort of butted in. "I know who it was, Freeman," he said. "It was George's Tom, guaranteed, I heard him say he had a load of lumber to sell."

There was a pause as other people came into the shop. They were all enjoying the show. Freeman held up his hand for Harold to be quiet. "No, it wasn't George's Tom. They used most of their lumber, and what they didn't use they sold to Bight Tom."

Bill took the cigarette from his mouth and was about to roar with laughter. But instead, he squinted his nose and with a grin on his face yelled, "Who in the name of God is Bite Tom?"

"That's Tom Cassell, he lives up in the Bight, you know the cove further up around shore. Ever since he was a boy everyone called him that. They didn't want to get him mixed up with the rest of the Toms, so they called him Bight Tom. Mr. Newhook, he's not the Tom Mr. Drover was talking to because, if he was, he would have told him who he was. Bight Tom is a Tory. He's definitely not a Joey man," said Freeman with a grin.

With that, Bill Newhook roared with laughter and so did the rest of the crowd. Sam Drover sat with his elbows on the counter, resting his head in his hands. "How in the devil's name can I straighten this out?" he asked, as he looked up at Freeman and Harold.

Freeman winked at Bill and replied, "There's no problem to straighten out the Toms up in Hooping Harbour, Mr. Drover. Just bring in Joey, the barrelman."

Even Sam Drover roared with laughter then. He knew darn well he was being had.

P.S. For those who don't know, Joey Smallwood hosted a radio program called The Barrelman, beginning in 1937.

P.P.S. Premier Joey Smallwood never set foot in Hooping Harbour and neither did Sam Drover.

The St. Roch

CHAPTER
1

One afternoon I again sat chatting with Dr. Baxter Gillard in his living room. We were discussing a few facts regarding a new book I was writing when I noticed a peculiar looking picture on his wall.

He saw me staring at it and knew I was curious.

"I notice you have been glancing at that object on the wall," he said with a grin. "You probably think it's a picture but it's not, it's a tray."

"There must be some important reason for you to have a tray hanging on you living room wall," I said.

"There certainly is," he said as he went and took it down and put it on the coffee table. Then sitting back comfortably in his easy chair he said, "I'll tell you the story."

****

As you know, for the past few winters my wife and I have been going to stay with my daughter in Surrey, British Columbia. One afternoon five years ago my daughter's boyfriend, Charley, a well known federal employee in the diplomatic field, asked me if I would like to go for a drive to see something special. I said of course and we began driving through the streets of Vancouver looking at the different sights along the way. I knew Charley had me sized up to be just another old time Newfoundlander who sometimes talked too much and was not to be paid too much attention to.

'I'm going to show you something, Dad, that you have never seen before,' he said. 'It's down at Vanier Park on English Bay.'

Charley, who was from Vancouver, always called me dad, right from the first time he met me. Anyway, we came to the entrance of Vanier Park, which Charley told me was home to the Vancouver Maritime Museum, paid our money and went inside. As we drove through the park the scenery was spectacular. A couple of times I thought about asking if we were going to stop but I didn't. I just kept quiet. Finally, in the distance I could see something that resembled a vessel, and by golly, it was a vessel and a big one at that. There was a lot of traffic parked nearby and it appeared to be a popular tourist attraction. We drove closer. 'This is the *St. Roch* (pronounced Saint Rock) a boat I want you to see,' said Charley.

I looked at the vessel, especially noting its strange shape. I repeated the name to myself. 'The *St. Roch*, yes, the *St. Roch*.' I knew I had seen it before, but I didn't say anything.

Charley went on to say, 'Dad, I know you are used to boats, but you've never ever seen one like this in your lifetime, and never one that's so important.'

I kept quiet.

'There are lots of tourist going aboard. We might be in time for the start of the presentation,' said Charley, as if he didn't know the time it started.

Again, I said nothing.

'We'll go to the presentation; I'll buy the tickets,' said Charley.

We were met at the door and escorted to the dining area
where the tables had been removed to make way for more
seats. Two chairs were found for us on the right side of the
aisle about midway up. I figure there were forty to fifty
people in attendance. I sat there staring at the walls and
going back in my memory to the fall of 1942.

At the scheduled time, a man who introduced himself
as a guide came into the room and welcomed everyone
then began the lecture.

'Ladies and gentleman, welcome aboard the motor
vessel *St. Roch*, she is a jewel in the crown of Canada's
maritime history and unlike any other vessel that ever
sailed under the Canadian flag.'

He went on to tell in detail how the *St. Roch* departed
Vancouver in the summer of 1940 for a non-stop voyage to
Halifax, Nova Scotia. She went all the way through the
Arctic, commanded by twelve RCMP personnel and an
Inuit guide and his family. RCMP Captain Henry Larsen, a
Norwegian born Canadian, was in charge.

The guide related some of the close calls the ship
experienced going through several runs with a boiling tide
making it go twice its normal speed and pushing it so close
to land you could almost pick berries off the low brambles.
He also told about icebergs foundering so close it covered
the ship with spray. Everyone listening was spellbound.

It was a very interesting lecture until, he said, this
vessel left Vancouver with enough supplies aboard that it
didn't need to put into any port for anything, and it didn't.
He said the ship and its crew got their supply of water from
melting Arctic ice. Their aim was to make the trip in one
season, and they did. He said, according to the records, the
St. Roch went from Vancouver, British Columbia, to
Halifax, Nova Scotia, without calling into a single port. I
sat there taking it all in, and as I listened I knew the guide

was never informed about what I knew and I wasn't intending to let it pass.

'Excuse me, sir,' I said finally, 'I don't think you are familiar with the true information about the voyage of this vessel in 1942. A certain part of what you're saying is wrong.'

Charley, who was sitting close to me, was alarmed. He put his finger to his lips and hushed me to be quiet. He didn't want to be embarrassed. 'Dad, Dad, please be quiet,' he said. I think he was about to apologize for my interruption.

'Who is that man down there?' the guide asked and he didn't sound friendly as he pointed to me.

'I'm Dr. Baxter Gillard from Englee, Newfoundland,' I said.

Everyone turned and looked at me.

Before I could say another word he said, 'Dr. Gillard, if there is something we are not aware of about the voyage of the *St. Roch* in 1942 then we invite you to come and share it with us please.'

'I certainly will,' I said.

I walked to the front and introduced himself. I have to say I have no problem talking to an audience, having spent many years as a lay reader with the United Church of Canada in Englee.

'Ladies and gentlemen,' I said, 'I don't mean to be rude, however it's best for folks to know the truth because there may be people listening who are familiar with the real facts the same as I am. I don't want misleading rumours to spread and that is why I like to correct people's mistakes.'

'It's all yours, Doctor,' said the guide and I began the story.

CHAPTER
2

It was a bitterly cold afternoon in October 1942. The wind was blowing from the northwest at a stiff breeze. Navigation had closed for the season as far as the coastal boats or freighting vessels calling into Englee. All passenger and fishing boats were taken from the water and stored for the winter. In fact, the bight was filled with slob ice and slush. The ocean was freezing up. No one was expecting any vessels.

Charley Hopkins, one of the employees of John Reeves Limited, suddenly saw a strange looking vessel pushing its way through the ice towards the company wharf . He ran to the upstairs office of the manager, Baxter Gillard, that's me, and told me to look through my window at the strange looking boat coming in the harbour. I stepped to the window and sure enough, a vessel was coming into the harbour and heading for our wharf. I knew it wasn't a sealing ship as it was too early in the season for sealing ships.

I usually received a wireless telegram advising of the arrival of any vessel, especially if there was an emergency. However, with the Second World War raging, German submarines were being sighted in our waters and I thought maybe this vessel was connected to the military. Perhaps it was a mine-sweeper.

I picked up my binoculars, adjusted them and looked

closely at the vessel. *'The St Roch,'* I said, loud enough for
Hopkins to hear. I looked to the top of the mast and saw a
strange flag flying. I put down the binoculars and reached
for a book that identified marine flags of the world. I
quickly scanned through the British flags without any luck
and I knew it wasn't an American or German flag.

It was when I went to the C section, Canada, that I
found she was flying a Canadian flag. I told Hopkins and
said the vessel must be having some trouble or it wouldn't
be in Englee at this time of year. Hopkins said maybe a
German submarine was after the ship and I said he could
be right. We looked at the vessel for a few minutes and then
I told Hopkins to go down and catch the lines and see why
they were docking. I watched the vessel tie up before
returning to my paperwork. I had just started looking at the
ledger when the door suddenly opened and a man in
uniform entered.

'I would like to see the manager,' he said in an almost
panicky voice.

'I'm the manager, you must be from the Canadian
vessel *St. Roch,*' I said.

'Why yes, I am,' he said, a bit surprised that I knew the
name of his vessel and her identity.

I noticed he had an accent and it wasn't French.

'What can I do for you, sir?' I asked.

'I'm Captain Henry Larsen out of Vancouver, British
Columbia. We just came through the Northwest Passage on
our way to Halifax, Nova Scotia. This is our first port of
call since leaving Vancouver, and I wouldn't be here now if
we hadn't had an accident with our fuel supply.' Captain
Larsen looked worried. 'We were near Grey Islands when
we decided to switch to our last fuel tank. However, to our
horror, we found it completely empty. Either it wasn't filled

or someone aboard sabotaged it.' Captain Larsen was so
stressed he had to sit down.

As he sat down, I noticed the shoulder epaulets on his
uniform. They read R.C.M.P. and I knew what it stood for.
I had heard and read about the Canadian Mounties but had
never seen one before. I wondered what this Mountie was
doing aboard a vessel so late in the season, racing ahead of
the slob ice on the northeast coast of Newfoundland.

'I know it's no use me asking you for fuel," he
continued. 'You wouldn't have any reason to have any in
stock anyway. I suppose we'll have to get a tug out of St.
John's to tow us to a port that has a supply or bring us
some. Then again, the northern slob is heading this way
and there will soon be a solid jam of ice so the fuel
wouldn't even get here in time. Our plan was to go by way
of the Strait of Belle Isle but it's plugged solid.'

I smiled as I went over and shook Captain Larsen's
hand.

'You don't have to worry, Captain,' I said, 'all is not lost.
I have fifteen 45-gallon drums of diesel fuel that I have got
no use for. I can sell it all to you if you want it. Last fall I
ordered fifteen drums of kerosene oil that our customers use
in their lamps. But the supplier made a mistake and sent us
diesel fuel instead. The freighter was here two weeks ago
and put it off. We have no use for it so if you have fifteen
empty steel drums you can bring them ashore and roll the
full ones aboard. That is, of course, after you pay me.'

Captain Larsen could hardly believe what he was
hearing. This was nothing short of a miracle.

'Pay you,' he said. 'Whatever you ask I'll pay. You don't
really know how important our trip is. You see, it's a
voyage for Canadian sovereignty.'

I wasn't too concerned about that but after we talked

some more Larsen said, 'Come aboard, Mr. Gillard. I'll show you our vessel and pay you.'

We walked to the wharf and I told my workers to roll out the fifteen drums of fuel while I went aboard to get paid. After I got the payment in cash, Captain Larsen asked me if I wanted a drink of rum. I said no, but agreed to have a cup of coffee with him instead.

We went to the dining room and sat at the table used by the captain and first officer. Now, there were three tables in the dining room, the captain and his three officers sat at one, the other eight personnel sat at the other two tables. Captain Larsen said there were a total of twelve people aboard.

The cook brought two trays of coffee and fruit cake and placed everything on the table. When we finished the coffee, Captain Larson called the second officer and told him he was giving me a gift in appreciation for helping them with fuel to continue their journey.

'Mr. Gillard,' he said, 'the tray you have in front of you has a picture of our vessel on it. There are twelve trays, one for each member of the crew, and I would like you to accept one as a token of good will from Canada and to hang it on a wall in your office. You know, this vessel may go down in history some day.'

'I think it has already gone down in history as the first foreign vessel to come in Englee so late in the season,' I said. We all shook hands and I left the *St. Roch* with the tray wrapped in a towel. The ship slipped its lines and backed away from the wharf. It gave three long blast from its horn, saying thank you, as it moved out of the harbour and disappeared from my life forever, or at least until now.

After the *St. Roch* left Englee I went to my office with the tray. Just before I reached the office the outside manager Martin Barnes came barging in, he was on the verge of panic.

'Bax,' he said, 'I think you have made a big mistake by selling that vessel the fuel.'

I asked why.

'Did you recognize the captain's accent?' Martin could hardly control himself. 'He sounded German to me. I've heard that accent before when I was in St. John's. They could be on their way to blow up nobody knows what.'

I stopped to think. Maybe what Martin was saying was true. I thought for a few minutes more then decided to go to the telegraph office and wire the Newfoundland Ranger in St. Anthony and request details about the Canadian vessel *St. Roch*.

In about an hour the Ranger wired back and confirmed details on the vessel *St. Roch* and Captain Henry Larsen, and I tell you we were relieved. I stand here today without any proof that what I have told you is true. The tray would be my proof if I had it in my possession. However, a few years later the business of John Reeves Ltd. burned to the ground, taking with it this coveted treasure.

I paused then and said, 'If you count the number of trays displayed on the wall you will find only eleven. The one missing is the one given to me by Captain Henry Larsen.'

Everyone in attendance looked at the trays on the wall and counted. Only eleven hung there. They all started clapping.

I held up my hand to silence them and said, 'This is a great event for me to be able to see this magnificent vessel again. You see, when I sat with Captain Larsen in 1942 I was thirty-two years old. Today I am eighty, this is my birthday.'

Everyone stood up. They clapped and cheered and

started singing, 'For he's a jolly good fellow.'

As I went to sit down a gentleman in the front row stood up and said, 'Just a moment, Dr. Gillard, this calls for a celebration. I am the manager of the Vancouver Maritime Museum. At seven tonight we have another information session like this one and after that I would like to offer you a special invitation to a party to celebrate this event and your eightieth birthday.'

I didn't know what to say first, finally I said, 'Thank you, sir. I accept your invitation if Charley will bring me here.' Charley agreed.

At seven that evening we entered the dining room of the *St. Roch*. It was all decorated, they even had a large birthday cake for me. There were more people there than earlier in the afternoon and I gave a lecture about the living conditions along our coast before and after Confederation. When I finished, the manager took one of the trays off the wall and presented it to me as a gift from the City of Vancouver.

****

The *St. Roch* was built for the R.C.M.P. in 1928 to serve primarily as a support ship for remote police outposts in the Arctic. It was built with a strong wooden hull, shaped to survive in thick ice. After twelve years of service in the Arctic, the *St. Roch* began her first and most important exploit, a west to east voyage through the Northwest Passage. The ship left Vancouver June 23, 1940, got frozen in ice until July 9, 1941, and finally arrived in Halifax on October 11,1942. The *St. Roch* was the second ship to navigate through the Northwest Passage, and the first to travel the passage from west to east. The voyage of the *St. Roch* demonstrated Canadian sovereignty in the Arctic during the war years and extended Canadian control over its northern territories. It is said too that *St. Roch* was sent to the Arctic so she could assist in the event of German action or occupation of Greenland. In 1944, *St. Roch* made a return trip through the Northwest Passage, arriving back in Vancouver October 16, 1944. In 1966, after the City of Vancouver acquired *St. Roch* as a museum ship, Parks Canada constructed a permanent indoor home for the vessel and, in 1971, completed a restoration to her 1944 appearance. Today *St. Roch* is the centerpiece of the Vancouver Maritime Museum.

Harold Randell

Harold Randell wasn't happy as he held his axe and struck the large pieces of Arctic ice several time. He was trying to beat the ice into smaller chunks to go into the ice grinder that stood just a few feet away from him. Harold was unhappy because he wanted to go out in the boat with his father and help haul the cod trap and salmon nets. But his father wouldn't let him go. His dad said Harold had a job to do. He had to work at John Reeves Ltd., grinding ice into the small chunks used when shipping fresh salmon to the blast freezers at Englee. As he beat away at the ice Harold was partly crying. He was also mad. His dad had told him if he could get the ice ground by the time he went to the trap Harold could come. If not, he would have to stay. Harold knew he wouldn't be finished in time unless he worked at top speed, so he was working away as fast as he could. A little while later he heard a noise.

"What's that, Herb?" he asked the boy working with him.

"Sounds like your father's motorboat to me," said Herb.

Harold dropped the axe and ran from the shed to the head of the wharf where he started waving and calling to his father to come and pick him up. But his father ignored him and went on out the harbour. His father didn't mess around. His boy had a job to do and he would do it.

Harold would get ten cents an hour for his work.

Harold was nine years old.

Herb Pittman saw Harold throw down the axe and run to the front of the wharf. Herb's job was to keep the grinder going; people packing salmon needed the ice. Herb threw in all the pieces of ice that were small enough for the teeth to grab and grind into smaller pieces. Only the larger pieces of ice were left. Herb's Uncle Herb Hynes was foreman on this job. Uncle Herb had raised young Herb from a baby after his mother died. Although Harold Randell and Herb Pittman were just nine years old, Herb Hynes was confident they could do the job. They had worked on the ice grinder before.

Hooping Harbour, in June of 1940, had a population of two hundred and fifty; it was a fishing village located on the east side of the Great Northern Peninsula of Newfoundland. The people of the little village made their living from fishing. There was no other industry. You either became a fisherman or a fisherman's wife or you moved out. There was no room in the community for anyone who wouldn't work; that was made plain. Every family had cod-traps and the usual equipment that went with them: trap boats, wharves, fish stages, salt sheds, drying flakes and store houses.

Hooping Harbour is situated approximately three kilometers inland from the roaring Atlantic ocean. The village was located on a flat plateau at the base of towering mountains not far from cliffs that went almost straight up. Although land was limited and houses crowded together, yet the men and woman grew enough vegetables near the base of the slopes to be self sufficient. Hard work was the mainstay of the village. It was often said that when a person could walk they had to go to work. At age nine, you were classed as part of the work force of the village.

The people of Hooping Harbour built good strong homes able to withstand storms that swept in from the north Atlantic and blizzards that swirled around them from the top of the high mountains and the open country.

If parents died leaving small children, the relatives would gladly take them in. So it was with Herb Pittman. His mother passed away when he was an infant and his Uncle Herb Hynes took him in and reared him to manhood. But young Herb had to work, it was part of the culture.

"School was finished for the season around June 10, 1940," said Herb. "I'm not exactly sure of the day but I know it finished a couple of days early because I had to go to work on the ice grinder. And the reason for that was because all the men and older boys were gone in the skiffs fishing. The fishermen were mostly after salmon because they were getting the best price for pound for it. And the ice grinder was working full time, grinding ice to pack the salmon in to keep it from getting soft before it reached the cold storage at Englee."

****

John Reeves Ltd. was a well known fish company along the Northern Peninsula during this period. The company was mainly in the salt fish business, exporting their product to the Mediterranean and the Caribbean Islands. Before the 1940s, however, they got into the frozen fish business. It was then that salmon became a very lucrative product and they exported it directly to the United States market. The area surrounding Hooping Harbour was one of the best places to fish salmon around White Bay, probably because of the deep water and the fiord-like coastline.

The manager of John Reeves Ltd. at Hooping Harbour
was John Randell. Whenever salmon was landed in large
quantities he was at the wharf supervising the operation.
He was responsible for having the salmon graded,
weighed, washed clean and packed in ice ready for the
collector boat that came in late afternoon. On this
particular afternoon, John Randell was at the shed on the
company wharf overseeing the operation and washing
salmon in the big puncheon tub. Jessie Randell was
working with him and Herb Hynes was foreman. Two
women were also working with them. All was well.

As young Harold Randell stood on the front of the
wharf and yelled to his father to come and pick him up,
Herb Pittman continued grinding ice.

"I picked up a chunk of ice, looked it over and knew it
was too big to go through the grinder," said Herb. "But I
figured the grinder might handle it if I pressed it against the
teeth by pushing on it, so I threw it in. As you know early
June in Hooping Harbour might not be very warm, and
especially when you're grinding ice, for this reason I was
wearing warm clothing. My aunt, who reared me and cared
for me as one of her own, made all my clothes and most of
my footwear. That day, I had on a homespun sweater over
a top shirt, and over that I had a denim jacket that pulled on
over your head and buttoned at the wrist. I was also
wearing a pair of woolen mittens while handling the ice.
After the over-sized piece of ice went into the grinder I put
my left hand on it and pushed on it with all my weight. As
you can imagine, there wasn't much weight in a skinny
nine-year-old kid. The grinder-teeth were jumping, trying
to grab the ice. I suppose that's what happened, my hand

slid off. One of the teeth caught the sleeve of my jacket. A tooth went into the hole above where it was buttoned and pulled my hand into the grinder. Before I knew anything, my hand was gone to the wrist. I can't explain it, the cutters cut off my fingers, then the middle of my hand, then severed my hand at the wrist. Then it started pulling my arm further into the grinder. I tried to scream but couldn't. As the governor cut in I heard the motor speed up to give it more power. My arm was sinking further into the machine. It was like a monster was devouring it. I braced my feet on the side, and put my right hand on the side of the hole and pulled back. By now, the teeth were almost grabbing at my elbow. Blood was gushing everywhere.

"The sharp teeth were entangled in my jacket. I pulled with all my might. I heard the engine slow down. The teeth were grabbing again, but I held my ground and pulled against the monster that was almost at my elbow. The motor gave a loud bang and shut off. I had stalled it out. I pulled my arm away from it and jumped back."

****

Herb, who is now seventy-eight years old and a retired crab fisherman, remembers the incident as if it was yesterday.

"Earl," he said to me, "do you know what I did after I pulled my arm away, or what was left of my arm? I turned around and picked up another chunk of ice to throw in the grinder. I don't know why I did it. It must have been a reaction or something. Then I threw down the ice and yelled to Uncle Herb, 'My arm is off.' When he saw me all he could say was 'My God.' Uncle John Randell was standing near the puncheon tub. It was half full of water and they had several salmon in it that they were washing.

When Uncle John saw my arm and the blood streaming from it he fainted with shock and fell headlong into the puncheon tub. One of the women lifted his head above the water before he took any into his lungs and got him out. It was a terrible situation. I was bleeding badly and there was no first aid equipment anywhere around the premises. Uncle Herb quickly grabbed my arm and applied pressure above my elbow. It was a job to know at first how much of my arm was gone. Uncle Herb had a look and saw it was in shreds near the elbow. The bones below the elbow were all broken, what was left of them, the flesh was all torn into shreds. Uncle Herb knew a lot about first aid. He had served on the battle fields of France during the First World War and he knew what had to be done to save a life. He needed something to wrap my arm in so he took the first thing close to him. A piece of cotton cloth hung on a nail near the shed door. The workers used it to clean their hands after working at the salmon. The cloth was full of blood and salmon scales, but Uncle Herb had no choice. He quickly wrapped my arm in it and tied it tight. Uncle Jessie Randell was also working there. He told Uncle Herb to take me to the midwife, Aunt Lew Cranshaw. He said he was going to go and tell her I was coming and make sure she was home.

"A man named Sunny Hancock lived in Hooping Harbour. Everyone said he could stop blood. It was said he was the seventh son of the seventh son. Someone yelled to go and get Uncle Sonny. Well, they went and got Uncle Sonny. By now, I was beginning to get weak and lose consciousness. As I was being helped into the house of Aunt Lew, Uncle Sonny arrived. He put his hand on my arm, rubbed it gently, and said a few words. This grand old gentleman was so sympathetic that he gave me confidence.

Uncle Herb took me into the house where Aunt Lew was waiting. She got a shock when she saw me. It seemed no one had told her I was coming. She was dressed in a long white apron, her hair was rolled up on the back of her head, and she was baking bread. They brought me in and sat me on a chair near the table. A lot of people were gathering around outside, mostly women and youngsters. A minute after I arrived someone came in and said Aunt Rowena was waiting and had everything ready to do up my arm. It appeared Uncle Jessie had gone to the wrong house. Instead of going to Aunt Lew's, he went to Aunt Rowena's. So off I was taken to Uncle Herb's house where Aunt Rowena was waiting. Uncle Jessie helped her with a large bandage she tore off a flannel sheet and wrapped tightly around the cotton Uncle Herb had put on. She taped it all up with sticking plaster. She didn't even look at my arm. She said I had to immediately go to the nurse at Roddickton and someone should get a boat ready."

Uncle Herb called for Ambrose Randell to get his skiff ready for the trip to Roddickton, twenty miles away. Ambrose was getting ready to go haul his cod trap when he was asked to go to Roddickton but he didn't hesitate. Extra gas was put aboard his skiff and immediately young Herb was put aboard the skiff. The men who came with him were Ambrose Randell, owner and operator of the boat, Uncle Herb Hynes, and Uncle Sonny Hancock. Uncle Herb and Uncle Sonny sat on either side of Herb during the 3-1/2 hours it took to reach Roddickton.

"I was experiencing terrible pain but the two men held me close all the way to Roddickton and that helped me," Herb told me. "We got to the sawmill wharf before dark. When we shut off the engine several people were there.

None of them knew we were coming; they thought we were visitors. One man knew Uncle Sonny and figured something was up when he saw him. 'Uncle Sonny, is there something wrong?' he asked. 'We got a young boy with his arm torn off in an ice grinder. We need to get him to the nurse right away,' said Uncle Sonny. The men told us where to go and accompanied us to the dispensary.

"On the way there, Uncle Herb told one of the men to go and get Roy Cassell. He was a World War One veteran, originally from Hooping Harbour, who had been wounded near Cologne, France, and returned home in 1916. Instead of going fishing, he came to Roddickton and operated logging camps. During the summer months he was operating a tugboat towing logs to the saw mill. Luckily, he was at home when someone came for him.

"The nurse on duty in the dispensary was Emily Blair. She met us at the door and had me brought into the clinic. She sat me in a chair near a small table. By now the lights were on and everything looked very bright. Nurse Blair removed the flannel bandage. I guess she got a surprise when she saw the cotton that Uncle Herb had wound around what was left of my arm. She lifted the edge of the cotton and peered inside. I can almost see her as she said, 'Oh my, that is a really nasty wound you have there, young man. It's better for me to leave it as it is. You have to go to the hospital at St. Anthony.' She went to a cabinet and took down two bottles of iodine. She lifted the cotton on my arm and poured one bottle down into the wound. I didn't feel it stinging; it felt as if she had poured ice water over it. She poured both bottles of iodine into the wound and that was it."

Nurse Blair put several bandages around the cotton and put Herb's arm in a sling. Herb was still wearing the clothes he'd worn while working, including his denim jacket. Nurse Blair told someone to get Roy Cassell and was told he was already outside. Roy came in. He knew Herb's father and the rest of his family. He assured Herb he was going to be okay.

"Mr. Cassell," said Nurse Blair. "I want you to take this boy to St. Anthony. I will keep him here tonight. You can leave at daylight tomorrow."

"I can leave now if you want, it's a pretty good night," Roy said.

"No, tomorrow morning will be fine. I'll monitor his condition overnight."

Roy said he would be ready in the morning. By now a lot of people were gathering because almost everyone in Roddickton knew Herb's father, Noah Pittman. He was a logging contractor at Great Harbour Deep and when people learned this was his son most of the men gathered to offer assistance. George Hall, one of the owners of the Saunders and Howell Company steammill at Roddickton, came and offered to pay the cost of the boat to take young Herb to St. Anthony. Years later, Roy Cassell would say 'George Hall paid me my wages while I was on the trip, I never lost an hour.' George Hall also gave Ambrose Randell a can of gas for his return trip back to Hooping Harbour. "Ambrose went to someone's house and had a cup of tea and headed back home," said Herb. "I don't know why because he had a large trap skiff. Maybe there was a lot of fish in his traps. It seemed that was more important then trying to save my life."

****

During the night, Roy built a wooden frame over the twenty-six foot boat and put a canvas sail around it. That

would help keep the wind and rain off young Herb and
make it more comfortable for the nurse, he thought. But, as
it happened, Nurse Blair didn't go with them. After the
nurse had bandaged his arm Herb was given a sandwich, a
cup of tea, and a cot to lie down on. None of his clothes
were removed, not even his rubber boots. Herb said the
nurse watched over him all night, but he didn't get any
sleep due to the pain. It felt like he still had his hand and it
was hurting him.

At 5 a.m. the steam whistle at the mill blew. This was
the wake-up call for the mill workers, also a wake-up call
for Roy Cassell, Herb Hynes and Sonny Hancock. It was
time for them to get on the move to St. Anthony with their
patient.

"Not long after the whistle blew the nurse came and
told me to get up from the cot because she was going to get
me ready for the trip to St. Anthony," said Herb. "She
asked me if I wanted breakfast and I said yes. Sometime
between six and seven Uncle Herb came and got me. The
nurse said she could not go with us, for what reason we
didn't know. We walked to the Saunders and Howell wharf
and got aboard Uncle Roy Cassell's boat."

It was a cloudy morning. George Hall told Roy to go to
any merchant along the coast, get whatever he needed,
charge it to his company, and bring him back the bill.

"I think we are going to have the wind northeast; the
sky looks that way," said Herb Hynes.

"This boat can't take too much wind, but she's got to get
to St. Anthony regardless of the wind," said Roy.

Several men waiting to go to work in the mill were
there to see them off. It took the small motor boat two
hours to reach Englee, a distance of ten miles. On arrival,
Uncle Herb and Roy went to the wharf of John Reeves Ltd.

This was the headquarters of the company young Herb was working for. Herb stayed with Sonny, while his Uncle Herb and Roy went to see John Reeves, owner of the company, to say they needed gasoline for the engine. John Reeves told them to take whatever they needed. He said not to spare anything. Herb and Roy took aboard a drum (45 gallons) of mixed gasoline and a box of food and left. It was 10 a.m.

By the time the boat got outside of Englee and headed in a northeasterly direction the wind was beginning to pick up and it was raining.

"They had a mattress put on the floor of the boat for me to sit on, this helped somewhat, but it was a very rough ride," said Herb. "Uncle Sonny sat close to me all the time as we headed into the rough seas. By the time we got halfway to Conche the waves were eight or ten feet high. Uncle Roy was at the tiller, all battened down with his rubber clothes, he had a cape-ann tied under his chin."

The motor boat punched its way along the coast till it got close to Conche; the wind was increasing and the waves much higher. They got in the shelter of Fox Head and slowed the engine almost to a stop. Herb heard his Uncle Herb and Roy talking about the rough sea they could experience going around Cape Fox. Roy said it was pretty wild out there but they had to give it a try and it might get better after they got past Crouse. And go on they did. The little boat battled its way till four in the afternoon when the wind turned to gale force and the engine didn't have the power to push the boat into the wind any further. They decided to go into Northeast Croque Harbour.

Croque Harbor is a very important place in the history of early explorers. During the mid-1700s, Sir Joseph

Banks, the world renowned naturalist, set up his
headquarters at Croque Harbour and did a three year study
of land and sea mammals. His expedition consisted of four
ships and eighty-seven men, who built dwellings and lived
on land in the exact place where the little village of
Northeast Croque once stood.

It was very calm in the harbour. The boat tied up and
immediately people started coming to see who was there.
A Mr. McGrath brought young Herb to his house and his
wife looked after the boy as if he were her own son. She
wouldn't let anyone touch the bandages for fear of
bleeding.

The three men with Herb stayed at Mr. McGrath's
house and the women of the community cooked a meal for
them as if they were royalty. During the night several
woman stayed up to keep an eye on Herb. Shortly after
dawn some men walked up on the hill with Uncle Herb to
take a look at the wind outside. It was still blowing from
the northeast but it had dropped some. A decision was
made to move on, or at least try to move on. Young Herb
was put aboard the boat around 7 a.m. and wrapped in
blankets. A crowd of people stood on the wharf and waved
to them and wished the boy a speedy recovery.

As the motor boat got further out of Croque Arm
towards the open ocean they again ran into heavy sea but
Roy was determined to move on. He battled his way to the
Fischot Island Tickle and had to watch his chance to get
through due to breaking seas. After getting through the
Tickle they went into the village of Harbour-de-Vue.
Young Herb was now in a lot of pain, likely due to all the
bumping around from the headwind they were
experiencing. They talked to some men on the wharf and
were told that it would not be possible to cross Belvy Bay

(Hare Bay). Roy said they had to do it. Residents of the community gave them a lunch and told them there was a wireless station in the settlement of Fischot Islands. Roy decided to go there and send a telegram to Dr. Curtis in St. Anthony, requesting he send the hospital boat *Marvel* to pick up the patient at Harbour-de-Vue. Roy waited for a reply to the telegram and when it came he wasn't a happy man. "Unable to send *Marvel* due to high sea, will do so when storm is over."

They left Fischot Islands and returned to Harbour-de-Vue. As Roy was coming into the harbour he noticed the wind was dropping. He said he thought they should try getting across the bay. If they got across they might be able to hug the shoreline and get to St. Anthony before dark.

The others told Roy it was useless to even try. They said there was too much sea. Roy ignored them. Young Herb was put aboard the boat again and off they went in an attempt to cross Belvy Bay. The boat only got part of the way across when they had to retreat. The engine wasn't strong enough to push the boat against the wind. They decided to go back to Fischot Islands and while they were turning the boat it almost capsized. The group stayed all night at Fischot Islands. Just before dark the wind changed to the southwest and blew a gale; it also cleared up. An old man on the island who predicted the weather told them there would be a change in the wind before daylight. He said they were going to have a gale of northwest wind and it would come on with the sunrise. Roy said in that case there was only one thing to do and that was to get ready to leave before daylight so they could be across before the wind came on. The old man said that wouldn't be any good because the wind was blowing a gale from the southwest and there would be heavy seas across on that side of the bay. He said they'd need a big boat to get to St. Anthony. Roy Cassell decided that no matter what he would be heading for St. Anthony in the morning.

At the crack of dawn, Roy left the wharf at Fischot Islands. He planned to trim the west side of Belvy Bay in as far as the Springs or maybe as far as Brents Island. He would then head straight for Ireland Bight or Goose Cove. He hoped to get around Goose Cape before the sea got too rough. If he could accomplish that, he could keep close to the land between Goose Cove Cape and Fishing Point. He figured he would have shelter till he went around Fishing Point. It was a long distance in around Belvy Bay. The motor boat could only make five miles per hour at the best of times with no wind, however, when the northwest wind came on they had fair wind. When they passed by Ireland Bight, Roy told Herb Hynes they would have to go into Goose Cove due to high seas. Herb said there wasn't much use going into Goose Cove. He said they might as well take a chance and go around Goose Cape. Herb said they were out in it now and might as well stay out. Roy agreed. Uncle Sonny was sitting on the mattress in the bottom of the boat with young Herb. He couldn't see what was going on outside, but he was aware it wasn't good as they were being tossed every which way. Roy slowed the engine to half speed as the motor boat ran with the heavy seas. Due to the fact that the wind had been southwest all night and a heavy sea had pounded Goose Cape there was a lot of undertow boiling from the rugged coast line. In fact, everything was foaming for more than a hundred yards offshore.

Roy Cassell and Herb Hynes had seen action on the battlefields of France, but still their hearts were in their mouths as they came around the Cape. The wind and seas tossed them around like paper cups as they hugged the coast line, swirling every which way in the undertow. But they made it all the way to Fishing Point. Wes Pynn blew the foghorn when he saw them, Wes knew there must be an emergency for a small boat to be out on a blowy day like this. As they rounded Fishing Point the boat had a head wind all the way to the mission wharf.

"It was after 6 a.m. when we got to the mission wharf," said Herb. "No one was there to meet us. I suppose no one was expecting us; there was too much wind for the large boats to travel, let alone a small twenty-six foot motor boat. Uncle Herb put me up on the wharf. I could barely stand, my knees were wobbly. Uncle Roy and Uncle Herb got on each side of me and helped me walk to the hospital. When we walked through the door Uncle Roy told the nurse at the desk why we were there and she was shocked. She called to another nurse in a room close by to come immediately. The nurse came out quickly and asked what was up. 'This boy has his arm torn off and needs someone to help him,' said Uncle Roy. The nurse, Nurse Violet, immediately sent for the doctor. It seemed like only a few seconds and two doctors were there, Dr. Curtis and Dr. Loomis. 'Get him in the clinic immediately,' said Dr. Curtis. A stretcher was brought, I was placed on it and wheeled into the clinic. 'Are you two gentlemen his relatives?' Dr. Curtis asked. 'Yes we are,' said Uncle Herb. 'We are going to get this boy into a bathtub,' said Dr. Curtis. I was wheeled into another room where a large bathtub was filling with water. The only thing Nurse Violet took off me was my rubber boots. Uncle Roy helped me into the tub. Except for my boots, I was dressed the same as when I was grinding ice four days earlier.

"After I soaked in the water for about ten minutes, Nurse Violet took the sling off my arm. Then she got the scissors and cut my denim jacket from the waist all the way up the front to the neck, and out toward the elbow on my bad arm. She cut the sleeve off. She did the same with the shirt I had on inside. After she soaked my arm for about half an hour they put me on a stretcher and wheeled me into the operating room where Dr Curtis and Dr. Loomis were waiting. I remember they checked my blood pressure and my pulse. Dr. Curtis said I needed blood immediately. They asked me if there was a relative with me. I said Uncle Herb was with me and they sent for him. Uncle Herb told the doctors he was my mother's brother. They said if it was alright they would test his blood to see if it was the right type to give me. Uncle Herb said he was satisfied to give his blood. Nurse Violet took a sample and tested it. She came back and said the blood wasn't any good, it was the wrong type. They told Uncle Roy to come in. Dr, Curtis asked him the same thing, if he was willing to give me blood, he said yes. The nurse tested his blood, she said it was the same type as mine. Dr. Curtis asked Uncle Roy if he was satisfied to give me some of his blood. Uncle Roy said they could take every stain was in him if it would save my life. Dr. Curtis said they couldn't take every drop of his blood and Uncle Roy told them to take all they could get. The doctors put a tube from Uncle Roy's arm into mine. I didn't know anything until I came to the following morning. I was in a comfortable bed with my arm bandaged and in a sling."

Herb had several operations to fix the bones that were crushed in his arm. He spent a full month on the hospital ward before he was allowed to go outside. He stayed in St. Anthony till August 25 and by that time he was anxious to go home. One day he went down on the wharf and saw a schooner unloading freight. He asked if it was going towards Hooping Harbour and a man said they were going to Englee. Herb asked if he could get a ride. The man told him to go and talk to the skipper and that's what he did. The skipper said if he had his clearance from the hospital he would take him to Englee. Herb went to see Dr. Curtis and got his clearance to go home. The next afternoon he arrived at Englee. He went to see Mr. Reeves who was happy to see him. Mr. Reeves immediately got a boat ready and sent him to Hooping Harbour with Charley Hopkins and Ern Compton. Herb got back home late in the night. The next morning school opened. It was the first of September.

Herb Pittman went on to live a full life. He started working when he was eight and lost his arm when he was nine. Although he had only one arm, he was never at a loss. He took his place alongside carpenters, building his own home, even dry-walling his house single-handed. He worked at logging and was a leading fisherman for most all his life. He made his home in Englee where he was a renowned citizen. While telling me this story, Herb made it very clear he had no bones to pick with anyone, even though he lost his arm while working in a very careless environment. He worked his way through life wanting and expecting nothing from anyone. Herb, we wish you all the best.

Hardship on the Trail

CHAPTER
1

Joseph (Joe) Hancock had been married for over a year. He didn't have a home of his own, but he and his wife had a bedroom eight feet square built onto his father's house, with the door leading to the kitchen.

On this March morning, thirty-year-old Joe was sawing lumber with a pit-saw, trying to get enough plank to finish the trap-skiff he and his brothers were building. His brother Roy asked him to go to the house to see what time it was, "It has to be close to dinner time; my stomach is starting to talk to me," said Roy.

"There's not much use going for dinner, there's nothing to eat," said Joe.

"Mother told me last night she was going to cook some of them old pickled flat fish that's down in the stage, that stinky stuff we had for the dogs. Dad put them in soak a couple of days ago, they should be pretty good and fresh by now," said Roy.

"That's not bad, a smatchy flat-fish across your jaw," said Joe grinning.

"Tis better than nothing," said Roy.

"Wass goin to happen when all them old fish scraps is

eat. There's not much of that stuff left now anyway," said
Joe.

"I don't know. If there wasn't a jam of ice in White Bay
we'd row over to Fleur de Lys and get grub," said Roy.
Jumping down off the scaffold where he had been working
on the top end of the pit-saw, Roy brushed the sawdust
from his clothes and wiped his eyes with a piece of rag that
was on a shelf nearby.

"People are going to starve if something doesn't
happen. If the seals would only strike in, we might have a
chance," said Joe.

"As long as the ice stays in White Bay there's nothing
we can do about it. Men can't walk across on rough moving
Arctic ice, it's too great a distance," said Roy.

"Maybe we should head for the country; we might be
able to get a couple of caribou, or a few beaver, anything
to keep us from starving till the seals strikes in," said Joe.

"There's no use going in the country, the country is
cleaned, you know that, you had to walk almost to Sops
Arm to get a caribou a few weeks ago so that's out," said
Roy.

"Let's go to dinner, we'll have a talk to the old man,"
said Joe.

The two men went to the house where Fanny, their
mother, was cooking the salt flat-fish she had watered. The
smell made them even hungrier than they already were, if
that was possible.

"Where's the old man?" they asked their mother.

"He's gone in for a slide of wood," she said.

"What does he think of the grub situation?" asked Roy.

"You know what he thinks about it, starvation is staring
us in the face. It's like he told the minister last night, there's
no one to blame only ourselves. We should have had our

grub delivered last fall on the coastal boat, but now it's too late. We don't have an ounce of anything left," Fanny said as she took up the flat-fish on a large plate. "You're eating the food we had for the dogs and this is it."

"I lows before navigation opens, we'll be eating what's left of the dog," said Roy.

"You'll have to cook it yourselves, there won't be nar dog cooked in here," Fanny said.

Joe laughed. "Imagine, Mother, four big hulks of men in one house talking about eating dogs. Not me, though. I'll walk to St. John's for grub first, if I have the health and strength."

"If you're going to do it, it has to be pretty soon while you still have the energy," said Roy.

"I think I hear your father coming," said Fanny.

"Yes, I can hear Mark's stomach rumbling; they will be here in fifteen minutes," said Joe.

Roy started laughing. "You had better get your share of that dog grub before it's too late because when Mark smells food he'll clean up on what's here."

The two men took their portion of the fish. Fanny had cooked up a pot full of brown flour and corn meal that she poured over the fish. Each man had a half-cake of hard bread as well. This made the noon hour meal.

"I'll tell you what food we have left, boys," Fanny said with a sigh. "We may have a couple of meals of rolled oats left, three or four meals of beans and a quarter of a sack of hard bread. We've also got a slab of rusty seal fat for grease and that's it. I would say we have about a week's food left, and this is only the ninth of February."

Joe and Roy looked at each other; they knew something had to be done, no one could live without food.

Jim Hancock, their father, was a very stalwart man,

well respected in the town of Englee which had a population of a hundred people in 1907, with everyone trying to scrape a living from the ocean. Uncle Jim, as everyone called him, had a large family. Up to now the family had never known hunger or want. But due to the collapse of the fishery in 1906 the fish merchant refused to bring supplies to the coast that fall. Things everywhere looked very bleak; people were on the verge of starvation.

Uncle Jim was a very cheerful man; his sons could never understand how he could smile during the hard times. Mark, the eldest son, often told his father there was nothing to be happy about.

"You are alive, Mark, you don't have an ache or pain, that's enough to be happy about," his father would say.

"I have hunger pains, that's nothing to be happy about," Mark would respond.

Jim and Mark now came to the table. There were no chairs. They had stools to sit on but no one complained. After grace was said, the two joined in the meal and soon all the food on the table had been eaten.

"Father, you are aware of the food supply, I suppose?" said Roy.

Jim knew there was concern about the shortage of food in every home in Englee. The night before he had attended a meeting in the church to discuss the possibility of getting food somewhere. The only hope was either trying to get across White Bay or heading for St. Anthony where there was a Co-Op store, but St. Anthony was close to seventy miles away by boat, and getting there depended on the Arctic ice moving off.

"It looks like we may send a crew of men across the ice floes to Fleur de Lys, or maybe to St. Anthony if the ice moves off," said Uncle Jim.

"It won't be me going across White Bay on that rough ice. That's next to suicide," said Mark.

"Someone is going to have to go. If not, we'll have to dig a lot of graves before anyone gets their hands on grub," said their father.

"I know what I'm going to do,"said Joe.

"What's that?" asked Roy.

Joe thought for a few moments then replied, "When I was in the country about a month ago, I met up with four men from the Strait of Belle Isle and had a lunch with them. They said they were from a place called Flowers Cove. One of the men, Ike Genge, said Dr. Grenfell has a Co-Op started there, plenty of grub, a big store full."

"How can we get over there?" asked Roy.

"Walk," said Joe.

"Walk, who knows the way?" asked his father.

"I'll find the way across. This Genge fellow told me there's a river that runs into Canada Bay which flows out of a lake halfway across. He said when I get to the headwaters I'll only have to walk about two miles and take the open bog that leads straight across to the ocean. They have a trail marked and he told me what to do when I get to the big river," said Joe.

"You're not going over there, Joe," said his mother, "I'd rather starve first."

"How long do you think it would take you get there, Joe?" his father asked.

"I can walk from Little Harbour Deep river in two days with a caribou on my back. That's over sixty miles, and from what they told me it's about seventy miles to Flowers Cove, so it's not a lot more."

As they sat around the table they had a discussion about the food they had and how long it would last. They all agreed they had to make a move to get food, either they'd go in boat or walk, but right now they should start and make plans. After a long discussion, it was decided to send Joe to Flowers Cove in the Strait of Belle Isle. He could bring back a load of food and then they would see if it was worthwhile to send a crowd of men from Englee to get more.

"When do you think I should be leaving?" asked Joe.

"Right away," said Roy.

Their father held up his hand to get everyone's attention.

"This afternoon we will start getting Joe ready. He can set out tomorrow morning. He has to have enough food to last him for the trip across, and he'll need a good pair of snowshoes, also a spare pair, and he should have a spare pair of skin boots. The clothes he's wearing will be enough and another pair of socks," said Jim.

"Maybe another one of us should go with him, that way we could get twice the amount of food," said Roy.

"No, that won't be necessary. He'll be going on an experimental trip. If this trip is successful we'll send a couple of dog-teams right away," said Uncle Jim. They all agreed except for Aunt Fanny who thought her son would never be seen again, going to such a foreign place.

During the afternoon and evening they made a new pair of skin boots and an extra pair of snowshoes for Joe to take with him. The pack-sack he carried had special wide straps made from seal skin for easy carrying. In his pack-sack he had a piece of canvas to make a lean-to and one wool blanket.

****

In telling the story, Dr. Baxter Gillard said there was

nowhere in Englee where they could get enough flour to make bread for Joe to take with him. But Fanny went to the storeroom where they kept their meager supplies and searched the empty flour barrels, hoping to get enough to make a couple of pancakes for the trip. When she found none, she was downhearted. After she told Jim, he went to the storeroom with a hammer and tapped the barrels, causing the flour in the seams to fall out. He gathered it up and had enough to make two pancakes. He also cut off four thin strips of seal fat and made sandwiches. This was the food Joe would have for his trip from Englee to Flowers Cove, a distance of some seventy miles.

Everyone in Englee knew Joe was heading to Flowers Cove to see if there was food to be had. The big question was how would they get the food. No one had any money to purchase it from the Co-Op. And it would be next to impossible for any fisherman from Englee to ship his fish to the Co-Op in Flowers Cove during the summer for payment. Things were a little different with Uncle Jim Hancock. He had saved a little money as his sons fished with him. In those days the unmarried sons never received any money from fishing with their father and didn't expect to. Uncle Jim had sixteen dollars secured under lock and key in a cash box he kept under his bed.

During the night he got together with his sons to figure out what Joe could bring back. The first item they wanted was brown flour, a hundred pound sack. They also wanted molasses, tea, sugar, yeast-cake and rice. And Jim said, depending on what he could carry and how much money he had left, to try and get a few pounds of hard bread. Joe said he would have no problem carrying these items. His father said he would give him fourteen dollars. That would be lots of money to buy everything they needed and he expected there would be some left over he could bring back with him.

****

Everything was prepared for Joe's trip across the Peninsula.

At around eight o clock, Uncle Jim went to the home of Bill Canning. He was the person in town who could predict what the weather would be like the next day, and for the next week for that matter. Everyone depended on him.

"We are going to have quite a breeze of northwest wind tomorrow," Bill told Jim. "After that, we'll have a northeaster for a couple of days, but it won't be enough to stop Joe from going in the country. He's traveled in worse weather than we're going to have."

"There are camps along the way and he's taking a side camp and a blanket, so he should be okay as long as it doesn't get mild and begin to rain," said Jim.

"I don't think we'll have rain yet; the moon looked okay when it went down this evening," said Bill.

Jim was satisfied with the forecast as he headed back to his house.

CHAPTER
2

Joe Hancock got up long before dawn on the morning of February 26, 1907. He hadn't slept well during the night. He told his wife, Elizabeth, to stay in bed, saying he would have breakfast with his father. Uncle Jim had been up several times. He heard the wind howling when it started to breeze up shortly after midnight and knew a stormy day was coming. Bill Canning was right, but that would not stop Joe from going.

Fanny had Joe's breakfast ready when he came into the kitchen,. She had a large bowl filled with rolled oats and corn meal cooked together. There was no sugar, so she added a few precious partridge berries she was keeping to make a pie just in case someone got sick. She also had two slices of brown bread for him; there was no butter.

She whispered to Joe, "Try and get me a few pounds of white flour and a pound of raisins so I can make a couple of cakes for Charley." Young Charley Hancock had a crippled leg.

Joe sat at the table with his other brothers and listened to their different ideas about what he should do if a storm overtook him, or if he should run into a polar bear. He would carry the old Snider rifle in case he saw caribou and he could use that on the bear as well. He would also carry an axe.

****

It was blowing a gale of northwest wind with snow flurries. Visibility was almost zero on this early morning but now the eastern sky was starting to light up, indicating it was beginning to clear. For Joe, it was time to go. His plan was to go about three miles up Bide Arm to Glasberry Brook then take the trail and cross over to Canada Bay and head up the Tickles to Shoal Pond, then he would follow Crooked Brook back into the heart of the country. At a certain junction in the river he would find Eli Reid's trapping cabin and that was where he would spend his first night. If all went well he intended to have a noon meal at George Reid's house on Old House Point. For sure they had food because George had a farm and was self sufficient in almost everything. He would also have a meeting with Eli, George's son, who trapped the area between Canada Bay and Booney Lake. Eli was married to a half Micmac Indian girl, Wilhelmina (Nene) Bushey. They lived on Old House Point and she trapped and traveled the country with him. From Old House Point, Joe would go on to Eli's trapping cabin, about six miles inland from Shoal Pond. After spending the night at the cabin, he would cross over to Round Pond and follow the river to Booney Lake, then cross over to the flat boggy country, using a compass. (That compass is now in the possession of Kirby Hancock, a relative of Joe's.)

If all went well, Joe expected to arrive at Flowers Cove late on the evening of his third day after leaving Englee. His plan was to walk twenty-five miles per day. If he could do that he would only have to spend one night out in the open and that didn't worry him.

****

It was dawning when Joe strapped on his pack-sack.

"Are you sure you have everything you need?" asked Roy.

"No, there's one thing I forgot. I need to take some bank line (trawl line). I may need it if I have to reinforce the straps on my pack-sack or put lacing in my snowshoes in case the babyish (lines made from seal skin, which is what the snowshoes were filled with) chafe off," said Joe.

"I'm glad you thought of that. I'll get you some," said Mark as he ran to the stage.

Everything was ready and Joe set out on his trek across the Great Northern Peninsula. He started off on the ice near the family wharf; he had his compass in his hand and would head northeast up Bide Arm. His father and mother waved good-bye and in less than a hundred feet Joe disappeared in the drifting snow.

The walking was not bad going up Bide Arm, although the drifting snow made visibility next to zero. He made the three miles in good time while staying on course.

****

Joe Hancock grew up in Heights Cove near Englee. When he was a young boy he started fishing for cod and salmon with his father and brothers; he never went to school one day in his life. When Joe was twelve he was as responsible as a mature man. At sixteen, he owned his own boat and fished with his father. Joe became a country man. He was an excellent trapper and was the one who guided caribou hunters from the town of Englee whenever they went hunting.

Joe was a very strong man who could out walk anyone and could carry the second heaviest load of anyone in Englee. His brother Mark, said to be a giant, was the strongest men in the community. Joe married Elizabeth Cassell of Great Harbour Deep and they went on to have four sons: William (Will), Thomas, Norman (Abel) and Levi, and a daughter, Elizabeth.

As Joe took the trail near Glasberry Brook, the sun was peeking over the hills on the eastern side of Bide Arm, casting a shadow in front of him as he walked in a northwest direction. The drifting snow in his face slowed him down as he crossed the few open bogs on the way across the neck to Canada Bay. When he reached the shoreline, he found the ice unsafe to travel on and had to walk along the shoreline for two miles to the area called the narrows. There, he cut a hole in the ice and found it was safe to walk on. With the snow continuing to drift, he decided to cross over to the north side where he would be in the shelter of the heavy timber along the shoreline.

After Joe got across the bay the walking was much better although the snow was deeper. He kept up his steady pace and headed in a straight line for Old House Point. Joe arrived at George Reid's and was welcomed by the sound of dogs barking. A few came out and headed his way but a woman heard the commotion and called them back. George and three of his sons heard the noise and came out from a shed. Recognizing Joe, they waved their arms in greeting.

"There must be some important business going on for Joe to be heading this way so early. Someone must be dead or very sick," said George.

"We'll soon find out," said Eli. "He's half running."

Joe came off the ice and headed to where the four men were standing. He started removing his snowshoes.

"Joe, how are you?" asked George.

"The best kind, have e'r one of you fellows got a

watch? I want to see how long it took me to get here from home."

George called to his wife to find out what time it was.

"Half past eleven," she yelled.

"I had a hard tramp. The wind kicked up a lot of snow and it was drifting in my face all the way coming across the neck from Bide Arm. It was enough to cut the skin offa ya," said Joe.

"Is everything all right?" George asked.

"Yes, except everyone is hungry, hardly a bite to eat in Englee."

"We are starting to get short on a lot of things too, like sugar, tea and yeast. Dr. Grenfell's got a team coming through next week, they usually have extra stuff and we get some stuff from them," said George.

"I'm on my way across to Flowers Cove to get some food if I can find my way in to Booney Lake," said Joe.

They could hardly believe that Joe was walking across the Great Northern Peninsula to Flowers Cove to get food

"Are you serious, Joe?" someone asked.

"I sure am. We would have gone across White Bay to Fleur de Lys but there's a solid jam of ice in all directions. Can't even get out of the harbour at Englee," said Joe.

"I know," said George.

"We tried to get to Cat Cove one day about a week ago and couldn't get around Canada Head. It's been blocked ever since the first week in January" said Eli.

"About a month ago when the doctor came here on dog-team his driver, Jimmy Patey, told us it was the same wherever he went around the peninsula, a solid jam of Arctic ice, the earliest they've ever seen," said George.

"Why did you come on this route?" asked George.

"What do you mean by that?" said Joe.

"If you had gone in to Beaver Cove, you could have gone across the neck to Devil's Cove Pond and taken the lead all the way in to Clouds Pond, then cut through to the Tickles and on up to Shoal Pond. That would have been a straight line, but instead of that you went about five miles out of your way," said George.

"I wasn't sure if the ice was safe to cross over. It didn't look too good to me," said Joe.

"There's plenty of ice out there, we were out there last week," someone said, just as Eli invited Joe to come to the house for dinner.

Joe was glad to get the invitation. The Reids never turned away anyone, their doors and hearts were always open.

"Yes, thank you," he said to Eli. "And while we're having dinner I want you to draw me a map of the route to Boone's Lake."

"That won't be a problem. I've been trapping in there most of the winter. Had Nene with me on several trips, did good with the fur," said Eli.

The two men went to the house where dinner was about to be served. Joe was glad to see Nene. She was a lovely looking girl who had married Eli when she was thirteen years old. They had no children.

"How's Elizabeth?" she asked Joe.

"She's fine, told me to make sure to say hello, we may come here Easter," Joe said.

"I'll look forward to that," said Nene.

While they ate dinner, Joe and Eli talked about two different routes to get to Booney Lake.

"The trail along by Beaver Brook is the shortest route from here, but if you go that way you'll have to stay in the open all night because there are no tilts that way. Our tilt is in on Crooked Brook," said Eli.

"What do you think? Which way would you go?" asked Joe.

"Dad said you were five miles out of the way, but that's not right because if you go from here to Wild Bight and cut through to Hynes Pond and Freshwater Trey-town, you won't lose very much. Have you ever gone that way before?" asked Eli.

"No, never in the winter," said Joe. "I've been to Shoal Pond in boat during the summer."

"Okay, that's the way you should go. I'll draw a map for you. All the way over to the north side of Booney Lake, from there you will find a marked trail up to the high marsh. I've been there, had traps there once. It's a hard place for snow, I took my traps up and wouldn't go back," said Eli.

"Yes, I think that's the way I'll go. Draw out a map and mark the place where your tilt is located," said Joe.

"Okay, I'll draw the map as soon as we have dinner," said Eli.

While they were eating, Eli told Joe to leave his rifle with him and Nene. He said there was no need of taking the heavy rifle all the way across the country, that it would only be extra weight for nothing, especially if Joe was going through heavy woods with a load on his back. Joe agreed. After they'd finished eating supper, Eli drew a map for Joe and Joe was on his way.

CHAPTER
3

Joe had very little trouble finding the trail across the neck to Hynes Pond then on to Freshwater-Trey Town. He knew when he reached the Tickles. The ice in the Tickles was safe to walk on although there were many places where the going was very tough.

When Joe reached Shoal Pond he noticed the sky was beginning to cloud over.

"It looks like weather," he said out loud. He estimated the time by the partly shining sun and figured it was maybe 3 p.m.

The snow was more like powder on the river. He saw the high wooded hills called Horse Chops looming in the distance.

As he walked up the river he kept a close eye out for the signs where Eli had trails cut around places where the river was always open. Several times he almost lost his footing as his weight made the snow suddenly give way and settle. From what he was told and Eli's map, he thought he should be at Eli's tilt by 6 p.m.

Joe kept a close watch for signs and kept looking at the map as he moved along. He was making no mistakes while trying to keep up a good pace. But several times he had to stop and study the river when approaching a waterfall and then he would find the trail and walk around it. After he walked inside for three miles he went on the part of the river that was fairly flat and picked up the pace. By what he thought was 6 p.m. he figured he was close to where he should see marks indicating the cabin was in the area. He slowed his pace and carefully watched for the marked trees. Eli told him he couldn't miss the tilt. He said there was a bucket hung in a tree close to the river. By now the sun had gone down and Joe began to get uneasy. If he didn't find the tilt soon he would have little daylight left to get his side camp in place.

All of a sudden he smelled something, he knew he was close to a camp; the stench of burning embers was unmistakeable. When he came around a short bend in the brook he saw the bucket hung in the tree; it was a welcome sight. The log tilt was snowed up quite a bit, but he saw a wooden shovel hanging over the door and got hold of it. He dug out the stove pipe and removed the tin can that covered the top. He had to be careful with the roof for fear of breaking the birch bark shingles. By now it was dark. Eli had told him where to find the lantern as he entered the door and sure enough it was in the very spot.

Joe took a match from his inside coat pocket and struck it. The flame showed him where the table was near the wall. He placed the lantern on the table, cranked the globe up, lit it, and hung it on a strand of wire that hung from the ceiling. The tilt was exactly the same as when Eli and Nene had left it a month ago. There was lots of wood and food enough to last a couple of days. It didn't take long for Joe to get the fire started. Then, he went to the river, cut a hole close to a large rock, and filled the kettle and pot with water. Nene had given him a loaf of bread and a salt dried codfish that he intended to cook. Joe started singing. He knew he would have a great evening meal.

****

During the night a terrible snowstorm came on. Joe heard the wind from the northeast roaring in the trees. Even though he was in the river valley he knew visibility was probably zero. But he felt secure in the tilt and was more than glad to have a roof over his head. It would be a cold night under a side tent. After supper he checked his snowshoes for wear damage, they were okay, the birch frames were tough. Joe had a comfortable night and kept the fire going. He had no way to tell the time except at dawn and when the sun was setting. The rest of the time he estimated.

He awoke early, lit the lantern, and had breakfast. He checked outside and saw it was still very stormy. Although he was unable to see very far in the drifting snow, it appeared a lot of snow had fallen. As it began to get light he thought about what he should do.

If he moved on in the storm following the trail Eli had marked out for him on the map, he would soon be to the point on Booney Pond where he had to go in a northerly direction over the ridge to the high marsh. He would then be in an area not showing on the map. Joe wasn't afraid of the stormy weather, but he was in an area where he had never been before, an area where there were a lot of brooks so he decided to wait before making a move.

He had met some hunters a couple of winters ago by the name of Pelley. They were from Main Brook in Hare Bay and they talked about a large river called Salmon River which flowed from the high country not far from Booney Lake. In fact they used the same route as the people from Flowers Cove after they got to a place on the river called Rubes Steady. That's where Joe would have to get to and he would then be on flat country with mostly ponds and bogs. After it got light, he put his pack-sack on his back, left the tilt as he had found it, and moved out. It wasn't easy going up the ridge through the heavy timber; the snow was deep and got even deeper as he got onto higher ground. He came to what is know Godfrey's Pond and kept going in the same direction, north. He again took the timber area and came to High Mesh Pond then to the high mesh, a place the men from Flowers Cove had talked about. It was the main area where the trail took them to Flowers Cove. When he got to the high mesh he noticed the storm was beginning to abate. He took out his compass and studied it. He was on the right bearing, going north.

Flowers Cove is approximately fifty miles from the high mesh for anyone who knows the trail that links up the bogs and ponds. But for anyone who isn't familiar with the area it could be a hard task to reach the Strait of Belle Isle. Joe got his compass out and took a shot in a northerly direction along the bogs, then started walking at a slight decline toward Flowers Cove. He found the marked trail at the end of the first bog and proceeded through the heavy timber with his axe in his hand. While he was in the timber he noticed the sun was beginning to shine now and then and the wind had changed to the west. He thought he was going to get to Salmon River before having to boil up but that was impossible. Feeling hungry, he stopped at a small brook. He lit a fire, got his kettle from the pack-sack, and went to the brook. He could hardly believe his eyes when he saw the numerous trout in the water. He decided to try and catch a meal by using the kettle. He would boil the trout for supper if he got any. He went closer to the edge of the brook and leaned over, a mistake he regretted. The edge of snow gave way and Joe went into the brook halfway up his legs, filling his two boots. If it wasn't for him being so quick and nimble he would have fallen down.

Joe climbed out, cut some branches and sat down and quickly removed his skin-boots. He took of his wet socks and pants and wrung them out. He put on dry socks from his pack and wiped out his skin boots with a towel. The boots were beginning to freeze, he would have to hurry in order to get them on. But by the time he got his clothes back on the boots had frozen and he had no choice but to get out his spare pair and put them on. After his boots were on he filled the kettle, boiled it up, and had tea. Joe figured he had about three hours before making a side tent for the night. He knew it was going to be a cold night. He followed the brook through the timber until he came to an opening at the side of a large bog, where there was a small pond that was dammed off by beavers. He also noticed a lot of tracks of small game. "This would be an excellent place for trapping if it was closer to Englee," he softly said to himself. He crossed the pond and bog then went up a grade and came out on another large bog. Taking a look at his compass he saw the bog lay in a northerly direction. "This must be the big one that the Genges talked about, the one that led to Rubes Steady," he mumbled.

In the distance he could see what appeared to be a large opening. Going as fast as he could, almost running, he went down across the bog to the large pond on the river, this was Rubes Steady on Salmon River, the place the Pelleys from Main Brook had talked about. He suspected this was the camping ground where they said they had marked the trees. He searched for the signs they had cut in the trees. After a while he found the trees they had marked, one had BP engraved in it for Bert Pelley and he knew he was on the right trail.

Looking at the map he had drawn before leaving home, based on what the Genges had told him, he was certain this

was the place where he would take the trail going to
Flowers Cove.

He walked along the northwest side of Rubes Steady
till he came to a cut trail leading through heavy timber up
a hill to the large bogs. This area was later called Gap
Woods. Joe wasn't aware he only had to walk about three
miles to the end of the bog and take the trail all the way to
Flowers Cove. Because he didn't know he kept on in a
northerly direction which led him through a large body of
timber.

He had gone about a mile when he came to a pond in
the timber. Checking his compass he crossed the pond and
proceeded up another ridge. The going was not good, but
he moved on. A little later he came out on a bog on the side
of a hill. The sun was setting and he knew he soon had to
prepare for the night. As he stood looking in a northwest
direction, he could see what he thought was Labrador in
the distance. For sure that's the Labrador coast, he said to
himself. That must be the Strait of Belle Isle, it looks like
Arctic ice.

In the dying sunlight he took a shot from the compass
in the direction of the nearest coastline, and decided it was
the direction he would have to travel in the morning. He
made three chops in a tree, a mark for when he returned.

Joe was an expert woodsman, he knew how to survive
out in the cold, and on this evening it was bitterly cold. He
knew where to make camp and he had no intention of
putting his side camp up in the heavy timber. He had seen
people do that before and almost freeze to death. He found
a spot of black spruce about ten feet high, tramped a
narrow road into the center, and made a clearing. He
tramped down the snow and leveled it. He then cut a
couple of poles and stuck them in the snow. He tied one

pole across about six feet up. He figured the wind would change to northeast before midnight, so he left the camp open to the southwest. Taking a piece of canvas he had with him, he put one end over the cross pole and tied it down, then he unrolled it and tied the other end to another pole at a ninety degree angle in the snow. He cut small trees and made two sides; this gave him a three sided camp. He kicked snow along the sides to prevent any from blowing underneath. He cut enough firewood to last all night and stacked it close by. He cut branches to stitch into the snow for the floor, especially where he was going to lie down. He lit the fire in the front opening and filled the kettle with snow. About an hour after he put the kettle on he had enough water boiled for tea. He ate the rest of the bread and fish Nene had given him with his tea.

Joe took his wet socks from the pack-sack and hung then over the fire on sticks he cut. The socks were dry in about an hour. He moved most of the wood closer to where he was going to lie down so that he would be able to keep the fire going without getting up. He had everything ready before it got too dark. After he'd finished his meal he stacked wood on the fire, got his blanket, and lay down. In just a few moments he was fast asleep.

Joe figured he slept for three hours, or as long as the fire burned brightly. When the fire died down the cold winds bit at his nose, waking him up. Joe noticed the wind had changed from northwest to northeast. This was not a good sign; northeast wind was poison to someone traveling on snowshoes. But Joe wasn't too concerned. He was on the right track and he had enough food to last a couple of days if he needed it. After stacking the fire with wood again, he pulled the blanket over his head and went back to sleep.

When Joe awoke a couple of hours later, a major storm

was underway. The noise of the wind roaring in the heavy woods nearby had woken him. He was glad he had made camp in the thick black spruce, the storm wouldn't hurt him here, he thought. During the early morning Joe had quite a problem trying to keep the fire going due to drifting snow. He figured he had got close to five hours sleep and could now stay up for the rest of the night and keep the fire going if he had to. Joe knew the storm would be on for a day or two, but that wasn't going to stop him. He was in strange country and had set his compass course the evening before. The storm didn't matter. He was determined to make it. He would head out when it got light. Food was needed back home. He wouldn't let the people down.

At daybreak, Joe shook the snow and ice from the canvas tarp and with difficulty rolled it up and stuffed it in his pack-sack. After putting on his snowshoes and packing his gear, he stepped out of the camp area. A blizzard met him.

Joe walked into the heavy timber where the drifting wasn't as bad. He checked the compass bearing and the wind direction. This gave him a good angle to travel by. He would travel with the wind on his right cheek, that would put him in a northerly direction.

Joe traveled on, feeling good as he was on level ground. He was crossing large bogs, ponds and areas of timber. Using his compass, he kept to a fairly straight line. Sometimes he had to go around areas of woods with a lot of twisted birch and willow, but he made up for that when he got on the other side.

At around noon, or what he thought was noon according to his stomach, he decided to eat one of the pancake sandwiches made with seal fat. He stopped to take it out of his pack-sack and moved on as he ate. Joe wasn't particular when it came to food. The seal fat wasn't cooked, but it didn't matter just as long as it took away the hunger.

Whenever Joe came to a pond or lake he would speed up if the going was fairly good. He finally came to a large lake. He was at its eastern end and didn't know it was seven miles inside the Flowers Cove area. Before he crossed the lake he noticed the weather was lifting. That was good. Maybe he would be able to see the coast after he went through the ridge of timber on the other side. The lake was over half a mile across and Joe ran all the way. When he got through the timber and came out on the open bog he could see the coast. He knew within two hours he would be close to the Strait of Belle Isle and then he would be able to find his way to Flowers Cove. Joe shifted his compass course to northwest, which looked like the closest area.

After Joe walked for about an hour he came across a dog-team track heading in a westerly direction. He knew he was not more than three miles from the shoreline, in fact he could see Labrador in the distance so he decided to follow the tracks for a while to see if they turned to the coast. Not long after he began following the tracks he came upon a well used dog-team road going to the coast and immediately followed it. After walking for about a mile he heard dogs barking, a sign he was close to a community. Coming out onto the barrens not far from salt water he looked to the west and saw houses. He proceeded at a fast pace, keeping an eye out for people. It was now late in the evening and Joe knew it would soon be dark.

The small village Joe came to was Pines Cove, fifteen miles northeast of Flowers Cove. As he entered the village dogs started barking loudly. He saw a man coming from a shed and waved to get his attention. Joe knew this wasn't Flowers Cove. He could only see about ten or a dozen houses and he'd heard Flowers Cove was a much bigger place. The man, who had a long grey beard which reached down to the wide belt he wore, waved for Joe to come closer.

"Good evening, sir," said Joe.

"Good evening," replied the man as he held out his hand.

"I'm Joe Hancock from Englee."

"William Crane," was the man's reply.

"What place is this?" Joe asked.

"This is Pines Cove."

"I'm on my way to Flowers Cove. Could you give me some directions?" Joe asked.

"Yes, sir. The way you're going now leads to Flowers Cove. It's about fifteen miles away."

"Fifteen miles?" said Joe "Is there a marked trail leading all the way?"

"Yes, I would say there is. There are lots of trails from town to town between here and Flowers Cove. Are you going on there tonight?"

"I'm not sure, it all depends on the darkness. I may camp somewhere along the trail. I have a side camp and when I get to the thick woods I'll put it up for the night."

"No need for that," said William, " I have plenty of room at the house for you. Come with me."

William Crane and his family welcomed Joe into their home; he got fed and had a very comfortable night. He told them he had met Angus Genge while in the country and he was the one who told him how to get to Flowers Cove. "You met a good man. He has a store at Flowers Cove and he'll be glad to see you," said William.

During the night Joe told the Cranes and other neighbours who dropped in to see him about Englee and

why he was going to Flowers Cove. "We are all out of
food due to the poor fishery and the fish merchant not
bringing in enough food and supplies. That's why there's
nothing to eat in the town now. We usually go across
White Bay to get food if we're short, but there's a solid
jam of heavy ice blocking White Bay as far as the eye can
see," he said. "In the morning I'll get one of the men to
take you to Flowers Cove on dog-team," William told him.

"I won't be able to pay because I only have enough
money to buy food. If there's any cost I'll walk," Joe said.

"Don't worry, there won't be any cost because I'll take
you there myself. I want to go to Flowers Cove for
supplies, so I might as well go tomorrow. I have to stop a
few places along the way," William said.

Joe thanked him, he knew he had come among good
people.

Joe and William had breakfast before it became light
the next morning. Mrs. Crane had a lunch packed for Joe:
six slices of bread buttered with cow-butter and wrapped in
a piece of cloth. Joe hardly knew how to thank those kind
people. He was a stranger and they treated him as if they
had known him all their lives. Before he left Mrs. Crane
gave him a hug and wished him all the best.

"If you have any problem, my son, come back. We've
always got room," she told him.

William had eight dogs hooked up to his twelve-foot
komatik and soon he and Joe were on their way. It was 10
a.m. when Joe arrived at the Co-Op store in Flowers Cove.
He felt a little sad when William dropped him off at the
store. They shook hands and Joe thanked him for his
hospitality. He said many times afterwards it was almost as
if he had known the Crane's for a lifetime. It was, however,

the first and last time Joe and the Cranes ever saw each other.

Joe went into the store and saw it was well stocked with basic food supplies. Every shelf was filled with goods. The store manager was serving at the counter. He introduced himself to Joe because he knew he wasn't from this part of the coast. The manager knew every man from all the communities around. Joe told him who he was and where he was from.

"You walked all the way from the other side of the Peninsula to get food?" the manager asked in surprise.

"Yes, I'll take back as much as I can carry if you will sell it to me, sir," said Joe.

"If you've got the money I'll sell you all you can carry and more."

Joe took the note from his shirt pocket; it was wrapped and tied in brown paper along with the money. He undid it and passed it to the manager. Albert Rose, the manager, was a short stout man, with a pair of iron rimmed glasses hanging partly down his nose.

"You want a hundred pound sack of brown flour, there's no problem with supplying that," he said.

Rose pushed his glasses closer to his eyes and scanned the brown paper: four gallons molasses; twenty pounds sugar; ten pounds tea; five pounds yeast cake; twenty-five pounds hard bread; twenty pounds beans; ten pounds salt pork.

"We can supply all these items," he said, after reading the list.

"There's a couple more things I would like to have if possible, but I don't want them to show up on the bill because it's the old man's money I'm spending," Joe said.

"What would that be?" Rose asked with a grin.

"Mom wants some white flour and raisins to make cakes if there's enough money left over."

"How much of the stuff does she want?" Rose asked.

"Twenty-five pounds of flour and five pounds of raisins."

"You're going to need baking powder too," said Rose. "I can supply everything you need, we have plenty here. And, don't worry, the white flour and raisins won't show up on your bill."

"Make up the cost and I'll see if I have enough money," said Joe.

Albert Rose quickly figured out the cost. "Twelve dollars and sixty cents," he said.

"I have enough money," said Joe happily.

Joe counted out fourteen dollars and received his change. He knew his father would be pleased to have change. While Rose was getting the groceries ready he asked Joe how many dogs he had in his team.

"I don't have a dog-team, I walked over from Englee," he said.

"How do you intend to get this food across the Northern Peninsula?"

"Carry it across on my back," said Joe.

"Do you know how heavy this stuff is?"

"I don't know, maybe a couple of hundred pounds," said Joe.

Rose added the weight together then said, "Around 268 pounds, including the molasses."

Joe thought for a moment. "I can carry everything if I have a can to put the molasses in," he said.

"The molasses is forty-eight pounds. Each gallon weighs twelve pounds. Maybe you should leave it and take the rest," said Rose.

"No, I'll take it in a can if I can get one. The rest of the stuff I'll take on my back," said Joe.

Rose figured it out again. "If you take the molasses in a can you'll have to carry 220 pounds on your back."

"I'll take the salt pork and beans in one hand and the molasses can in the other; the rest I'll take on my back," said Joe.

"That will be one hundred and ninety pounds on your back plus your camping gear is another twenty pounds. That's a lot of weight" said Rose.

"That'll be okay," said Joe.

Rose said nothing more; he had to see it first. Joe put the one hundred pound sack of brown flour in his pack-sack plus the white flour and raisins. The rest of the stuff he put in watertight bags and tied it to each side. He tied his camping gear to the top of the flour bag.

"When do you plan to head back home, Joe?" asked Rose.

"As soon as I get a lunch I'm heading out."

"Let's you and I go to my home and have lunch. Leave your stuff here, it'll be all right. I'll get one of the clerks to draw the four gallons of molasses in a can; we have them here with good handles for carrying. I'll give you a can and he'll have it ready when we get back," said Rose.

"Thanks, that'll be wonderful," said Joe, as they left the store.

****

Joe had a great meal and a chat with Albert Rose and his family. Rose told Joe where to take the country trail going across the Peninsula from Flowers Cove. He said he would draw him a map before he left. Joe told Rose about his meeting with the Genges, and especially with Angus Genge.

Rose was surprised, "In that case you'll have to visit

Angus, he'll be the one to tell you where to go and put you on the right trail. Angus lives just across the road, his store isn't far from here. We'll run up to see him for a few minutes."

Angus was happy to see Joe but surprised as to why he was in Flowers Cove.

"Good grief Joe," he said, "you came all the way over here to get a back load of grub? You won't be able to carry very much. The going is pretty bad, and it looks like more snow on the way."

"I don't mind the snow. My biggest problem is following the trail. When I get to the lake on the big river I'll be all right. I came over here first to get familiar with the trail. Other people will come later if I tell them it can be done and we can follow the trail."

"That won't be a problem because the trail is well marked. After you get to Island Pond we have marks up that are easy to follow, even in bad weather," said Angus.

"I was just telling him, we should draw out a map all the way over to the Gap Woods. From there he'll go down through our trail to Rubes Steady on Salmon River," said Rose.

"That's a good idea, let's do it now," said Angus.

The two Flowers Cove men got paper and plainly drew a map in detail for Joe. They went through every mile, step by step. Joe watched and listened. He had a very keen memory. He'd learned how to read and write without ever going to school. His mother taught him at home, showing him words in her hymn book and Bible. Joe only had to see the words once and he would remember them.

"All you have to do is take a light load. Don't over do it and that way you'll be all right," said Angus.

"Don't be talking," said Rose. "He's already got his

bags packed and they weigh almost three hundred pounds, enough to make an ox stagger."

Angus laughed. "Albert, you don't know this man. He's the fellow I was telling you about a while ago. We met him on the open country one nasty evening on his way home. He had an old doe on his back, a three-year-old stag in tow with a rope around his waist, a compass in one hand and a rifle under his arm."

Albert Rose had nothing to say.

"I presume you're leaving in the morning, Joe," Angus said.

"No, I'm leaving right away. I should make ten miles before dark," said Joe.

"There's a dog-team path going into the big lake, that's five miles in. People are hauling firewood and logs and you'll have no problems following that path. The walking should be very good," said Angus. He paused for a moment then added, "I'm going to see if there's anyone going in that way, you could get a ride."

Joe said any kind of a lift would be great.

"You fellows go on back to the Co-Op store. I'll check around and meet you in about ten minutes," said Angus.

When Rose and Joe arrived back at the Co-Op, Joe said he didn't want to be a bother to anyone. He said he was satisfied to take his load and head out and that's what he intended to do.

"Just wait a few more minutes and see if Angus can find someone going that way," said Rose.

Joe didn't want to wait. He put the heavy load on his shoulders, took the molasses can in one hand, and in the other held a burlap bag containing the salt pork and beans wrapped in a rubber coat. Albert Rose later told Dr. Grenfell that when Joe Hancock loaded the food that he carried across the Peninsula to Englee the floor in his store cracked with the weight every time he moved around.

Angus arrived as he was going through the door. "Everyone is gone in the woods and won't be back till late. You should wait till tomorrow morning. You're guaranteed to get a ride then and you'll be just as far ahead," he said.

"No, I think I'll get on my way now. By the time it's dark I should be across the big lake and have camp set up for the night," said Joe.

"I'll walk in across the first bog and show you the right trail to take," said Angus.

"Thanks a lot, that'll be wonderful," said Joe.

"You walk on across the cove to that open place over there," said Angus, pointing it out, "I'll get my snowshoes and meet you over there in about ten minutes."

In a few minutes Joe stepped out on the ice in Flowers Cove harbour and was on his way to Englee, more than seventy miles away.

Angus Genge set Joe on the right trail. Joe didn't need his snowshoes because the dogs and the sleighs had the snow packed hard, but he kept them on anyway for fear of sinking with his heavy load.

Angus told Joe he was heading back. "You'll find your way from here," he said.

"Thanks for everything, Angus. If you ever come our way look us up, we'll have a bed for you," said Joe.

The two men shook hands, they would never see each other again.

CHAPTER
4

Joe was walking as fast as he could with the load he was carrying. He followed the trail marked on the map Ike had drawn; he was on track. The weather was very cold. The wind was switching to the northwest and if that was the case he would have to spend the night by the big lake, but maybe he would go on to Roses Pond. He met a dog-team about half way in, they told him he was on the right trail to the lake. As the wind picked up it was to his back and kicking up low drift. The trail was good when he came to the big lake. He knew where he had to go to take the trail on the other side and decided he would go on. By the time he crossed the lake it was getting late, but on he went. It was almost dark when he reached Roses Pond. He would have to put up his side tent in the dark. Putting down his load, Joe went to work preparing for the night. In about half an hour he had his camp ready and his kettle over the fire melting snow to make tea. While waiting for tea he studied the map. His present position was marked twelve miles. He had made it this far in good shape.

Joe ate two slices of the buttered bread William Crane's wife had given him. It was a treat to have it and he thought about how kind they had been to him, a stranger they'd never seen before. It was a very cold night with a high wind. Joe huddled near the fire with the blanket wrapped around his shoulders. He dozed a couple of times but around midnight the cold wind pierced through him. Although the side camp gave him some protection, nothing except a complete enclosure could keep out the swirling snow. This was his fourth night away from home. He thought about Elizabeth and the house they planned to build this coming summer.

Although the night was long and brutish cold with drifting snow, not once did Joe think he wasn't going to make it. In the early dawn, he walked out to the edge of the pond. He knew where he had to go after he crossed this pond.

Joe hung the kettle over the fire, melted the leftover tea from his evening meal, and took two more slices of the buttered and now frozen bread. He put the bread on a stick and toasted it over the fire. "Thank God for Mrs. Crane," he said as he ate.

He took down the side camp, rolled it up, and tied it on the outside of his pack-sack. In only a few minutes he was ready to go. Joe had a bit of a problem getting the heavy pack-sack on his shoulders as the straps had frozen. He put the straps near the fire and softened them up. He put on his snowshoes first and tightened the slings comfortably around his feet. He hoped to get to Eli's tilt before it got dark, but realized it would be almost impossible. He stamped a hole in the snow about two feet deep. This gave him a better chance to get the heavy pack-sack on his shoulders as he wouldn't have to lift it as high.

Joe walked at a fast pace across Roses Pond. There were times when he could hardly see his snowshoes in the heavy drifting. But as the map indicated, the trail was clearly marked at the edge of the pond. Walking through the woods was fair. At least he was sheltered from the heavy drifting, but he knew he would encounter high winds on the next pond. Island Pond was a large body of water over two miles long with many islands. The thing Joe had in his favour was the wind. As he started down the pond he was reminded of the slob ice that sometimes formed in the center of these large ponds due to the weight of snow. He pushed down his axe handle to see if any was present as he got further out. The two-foot handle could not touch the ice so he knew he was all right. He estimated it took over an hour to walk the length of the pond. When he got near the end, he saw his tracks from two days earlier. They were drifted hard and he wondered if he should follow them or go by the map his friends had drawn. This would not be a good place to get astray he thought.

Joe realized if he followed his tracks he would have to travel through a lot of woods where the snow was soft and deep. He had experienced that two days ago and with no load on his back he didn't sink much, but now with the heavy load things were much different. He decided to stick to the trail on the map; at least he would be following the open ponds and bogs. Visibility was zero at the end of the pond due to drifting. After searching around a few minutes he found the marks on the trees that marked the trail. He had problems getting off the pond due to high snowdrifts, but after he got into the trees visibility improved.

The sun indicated it was almost noon as Joe walked the open bogs. He had to walk in almost a westerly direction in order to get to the Gap Woods. He knew this was where he would pick up his own trail and maybe stay at the camping area from his second night. As he walked along he stumbled on a patch of ice. In trying to catch himself he fell near a drift bank. Joe knew at once he had done damage to the pack-sack as one of the slings came loose and fell from his shoulder. He examined the end of the sling and saw it was broken. The sealskin had broken near the loop at the end where it was sewn onto the pack-sack. Joe examined the other sling and saw it was tearing as well; the weight was too much. He would have to get in off the open bog to do repairs. It was too cold here. For now, he would have to use both hands to keep the pack-sack on his back. He put down the can of molasses and the bag holding the other items with plans to return to get them. Holding the top of the pack-sack with his right hand he went with the wind towards the woods a half mile away. It took him over half an hour to reach the shelter of the trees. He removed the pack-sack and stashed it near a large tree and hurried back to the open bog to retrieve the things he'd left there. When he got back he started his repairs. He got the trawl line from the pack-sack, cut off a couple of feet, and pushed it through the strap several times then tightened it. He would have to cut a hole through the pack-sack in order to secure it in place. In doing so he shortened the strap. The trawl line would now be on his shoulders and with nothing to use for padding he knew it was going to cause a problem as the trawl line would cut into his flesh. Once his repairs were done, he very carefully and with great difficulty put the pack-sack back on his shoulders. He then returned to the bog to get back on course. He knew he would have to do a major repair on the strap when he stopped for the night and set up his side tent.

It was quite a task walking into the drifting snow with the heavy load, but he made it. Joe had approximately three more miles to go to reach the Gap Woods where he would pick up his earlier trail and then he would go down to Rubes Steady and camp for the night. He found the Gap Woods and his snowshoe tracks in the dying sunlight. He would now make camp in the area where firewood was

easy to get. Joe found a suitable spot and set up his side
camp. Before it got dark, he cut wood enough to last the
night. After starting a fire and putting the snow-filled kettle
on to boil he proceeded to repair the slings on the pack-
sack. He used the pieces of cloth Mrs. Crane had wrapped
the bread in as padding around the trawl line on one strap.
For the other strap, he used his spare socks as padding. The
padding would certainly stop the trawl line from cutting
through his shoulders.

Joe did not sleep at all during the cold cruel night. He
kept the fire going and got as close to it as possible, but
even with the blanket wrapped around his shoulders he
shivered all night. He longed for morning. For breakfast,
he melted more snow and made tea and ate half the seal fat
sandwich his mother had made.

As the dawning broke, Joe knew from the look of the
sky that a storm of some kind was brewing. He managed to
get the pack-sack straps over his shoulders and proceeded
to walk the mile or so towards Rubes Steady. The going
was slow and his tracks were hard to follow in the trail due
to snow that had fallen two nights before. After crossing
the steady, Joe started walking up the long lower bogs
toward the high marsh. With every step he felt the trawl
line cutting into his shoulders. The 220 pounds on his back
felt like five hundred, and his right hand holding the wire
handle on the molasses can was numb and cold.

This area was the steepest uphill climb he had to make
and he thought when he got to the high marsh things might
get a little better. He came to the heavy timber area and
started following the brook. He was now able to step into
his tracks and the going was much better. Before he
reached the high marsh a storm came on. It was snowing
hard. He knew he had to try and reach Booney Lake by

mid-afternoon in order to get to Eli's tilt before dark. He wasn't worried about getting to the tilt even if it was after dark. Before leaving he'd cut enough kindling to start a fire and enough wood to last all night in case he was late arriving on his return trip. As Joe came out on the bottom end of the high marsh visibility was next to zero. But he knew where he was and the direction he had to go and even though the wind was blowing he could still see his tracks. Joe trudged along at a slow pace making sure his snowshoes were on the hardest snow. He didn't want to stumble and fall. He was afraid that could break the fragile straps on his pack-sack.

After a terrible struggle Joe made it to the top of the high marsh. His mustache was caked in ice and he had icicles on his eyelashes. After he entered the heavy woods and started moving downhill toward Booney Lake he could move a little faster; he was away from the drifting snow. It was three miles down to Booney Lake and Joe made good time compared to when he was on the high marsh. Although he lost his tracks among the timber he knew he was going in the right direction, downhill to the lake. The wind was northeast, blowing down the pond. Joe would be heading into the wind as he struggled along. With darkness coming on, he figured he had two hours to get down the lake, cross the two steadies, and go up across the large bog before taking to the timber to go down to Crooked Brook where Eli's tilt was. At the end of Booney Lake, he switched the load he carried in his hands, but the load on his back was the same. He had a problem getting off the lake because of heavy snow drifts. He cut through the timber to the first steady and hurried across it. Visibility was a little better as he neared the second steady, although he was still heading into the wind. Joe kept up a stiff pace as he went to the next steady where he turned to the right and headed in a southeast direction. He was pleased the wind wasn't in his face any longer. It would soon be getting dark and he had to get to the end of the open bog. If he got there he would make it to the tilt, although the pain in his shoulders was almost too much to bear.

Joe's arms were aching and his fingers on the molasses can hanger were numb, but he couldn't stop. He wanted to get to the tilt. He didn't want to spend this stormy night huddled under the side tent, less than two miles from a bunk. He finally got to the end of the bog and found the tree he had marked. It was all downhill from here except for the two small bogs he had to cross. With his shoulders aching, Joe walked through the timber. He knew where he was, he could see the form of his tracks in the twilight as he struggled through the snow. The tilt was near; he saw the area where he had cut firewood. The tilt was almost covered in snow with only the top of the can over the stove pipe visible. Joe tramped in the snow to make a place to put his pack-sack and removed it with great effort. Using his snowshoe he dug down to find the wooden shovel he had put back in its place over the tilt door. After digging the snow away from the doorway he opened it and stepped inside. He went back to get his pack-sack and brought it inside. It took only a few minutes for Joe to light the lantern and get the fire going, "This is heaven below," he said to himself as he filled the kettle and a pot with snow and placed it on the stove. He felt very hungry. He still had two slices of cow-butter bread left and half of the seal-fat pancake and that's what he would have for his supper. From now on he would eat some of the hard bread he was carrying. His plan was to soak some cakes overnight so that they would soften enough to eat the next day.

Joe's shoulders were in terrible shape. The flesh on his collar bones was chafed and bleeding. His neck and shoulder muscles had tightened up and his hands were hurting, especially the fingers on the left hand where he had been holding the can for so long. After he got settled away he checked his snowshoes and skin boots. His greatest problem was the slings on the pack-sack. There was only one solution. In the morning he would have to cut his blanket into strips and roll it around the slings to make a better padding. Joe was more than happy to be inside during such a stormy night. He had firewood and oil for the lamp and he had enough food under the roof to last him a full year if need be. He slept most of the night, waking only when the fire went down. When Joe awoke he didn't know what time it was, but suspected it was getting close to daylight. He opened the door to peer outside. Eli had a lifetime of experience building tilts and he knew it was a must to have the door swing inwards; otherwise if a storm came on in the night the person inside would have quite a problem trying to open it. When Joe opened the door he saw a straight wall of snow in front of him. He filled the kettle with snow and put it on the stove, thinking he would have tea and soaked hard bread. He wondered if he should partake of a little molasses. He had four gallons of the stuff, a spoonful in his tea and a little on the soaked hard bread would make a wonderful breakfast.

After breakfast he decided to start digging out. He pushed the shovel handle through the wall of snow but saw no light. Maybe it's not daylight yet, he thought, but he had to make sure. Joe dug a deeper hole in the snow and reached out with his shovel. When he pulled the shovel back he could see light outside. All was well, he would dig out. After digging his way out, he discovered the storm was still raging. But that wouldn't stop him. He would reach Canada Bay today supposing he had to crawl. But the first thing he had to do was repair the pack-sack straps so he could carry the load. Once he had the straps repaired with two strips from his blanket, he was ready to start out.

Joe secured the tilt and put the shovel back in its place over the door. He proceeded to put the pack-sack he'd bought out and laid on the snow up onto his sore and aching shoulders. Bending down, he slowly put his arms through the straps and carefully took the weight of the pack-sack. He tried to stand but couldn't. Pain shot through him. He tried again to stand but his shoulders couldn't take it. He had to get the load on his back. It didn't matter how sore his shoulders were. The food had to go to Englee. He wasn't going to leave it here in the middle of the country, bad shoulders or not. He slowly and painfully took the strain of the load. He somehow managed to get to his feet. He picked up the can of molasses and the other package and struck out on the trail leading to Canada Bay.

CHAPTER
5

It will never be known what Joe Hancock suffered walking out of the country that day. Folks have tried to describe what he did but failed to find the right words. Immediately after leaving the tilt he encountered heavy snow on the brook he was following. His snowshoes could barely hold his weight. And, to make matters worse, a major blizzard was in progress with the wind northeast. Pain blurred his sight with every step he took. He told himself after a while his shoulders would get numb from the pain and that thought made him go on. Two miles after leaving the tilt the river turned to the southwest. This made the going a little better as the wind was now to his back. About half a mile outside the bend in the river there was a cliff on the eastern side. When the river flooded, water backed up there. If frost came on suddenly and it froze over, shell ice would form, creating a hazard for anyone walking on it, especially if it was covered with snow. Joe knew nothing about that. He had walked this way on his way in, but now he was close to 300 pounds heavier.

As he hurried down the snowy river and started walking near the cliff, the ice and snow gave way. For a second, Joe thought he was in the water. His first reaction was to fall ahead in a prone position; it would spread out his weight, slowing his descent.

"My God," he yelled, "I'm in the water."

The molasses can went one way, the package in his right hand went the other. He waited for a few seconds and discovered he wasn't sinking any further. As he lay there and surveyed his surroundings he immediately realized what had happened when he saw the sides of the hole he was in. "I've broken the shell ice and gone down into the dry brook," he said to himself. The weight on his back kept him from getting up. He had to roll over on his back and painfully pull his arms from the slings. The shell ice had sunk at least four feet. He could hear the faint noise of the brook but knew he was in no danger. He found the molasses can and the package and threw them out of the hole. He would have to tramp a road to get out with the heavy load. It took Joe more than half an hour to get back on his feet. He realized he would have to watch out for places like that from now on. Next time, he might not be as lucky.

Joe finally reached Shoal Pond. He estimated it had taken him six hours to get this far. He had reached the Tickles and he was quite familiar with the area. His family had lived one winter at Clouds Pond. The winter trail they used between Englee and Clouds Pond went to Pinnacle Pond, Devil's Cove Pond, and then out to Devil's Cove where they had their boat to take them home. Joe had no boat, so he decided to go to Devil's Cove Pond, then turn to his left and cut across the neck to Beaver Cove and cross Canada Bay. From there, he could pick up his tracks and head for home. That way, he could shorten his trek by about six miles. Joe kept going even though every step was a burden. His mind told him to stop and take the load off and come back with a sleigh but he still kept going. When he got to Black Duck Pond he stopped. The pain in his shoulders was awful. He had to do something and the only thing he could do was pad the straps of his pack-sack with more pieces of his blanket. He took off the pack-sack with great difficulty. He examined his shoulders and saw that his undershirt was stuck into his wounds. Dried blood was all over his chest and down as far as his belt. His neck was stiff and swollen and the knuckles on his left hand were swollen. He cut more strips from the blanket and wound them around the trawl-line. When that was done he put the pack-sack back onto his shoulders, crying out with pain as the straps set into his wounds.

When Joe came out on Clouds Pond it was twilight. He was going to have to stop for the night and put up the side tent. The wind was changing to the west, and he could see the rays of the sun on the high mountain on the far side of the pond. He was familiar with the area and decided to camp on an island he knew on Clouds Pond. It was after dark when he reached the island where the Hancocks once had a cabin they finally beat down for firewood. Joe wished the cabin was still standing. He made a little tea and ate the soaked hard bread for his evening meal. It was a very, very cold night and as the sun went down the wind picked up with drifting snow. It was too cold to sleep. Joe huddled over the fire and hoped for the best. He kept the kettle boiled and every few hours he would have tea. He put the molasses can close to the fire to warm it enough to run out. It tasted wonderful in his tea. Around midnight Joe had to cut some more firewood. Each swing of the axe made him cringe with pain. He dreaded the thought of strapping on the pack-sack in the morning.

"Maybe I could hoist it up in a tree. That would keep the wild animals from eating it, and then maybe Mark and Roy could come and get it," he said aloud. But then he added, "No I'm not leaving it. I'll carry it, or I'll die."

As Joe watched the stars in the morning sky, he knew Elizabeth and his mother would be very worried about him. He had been gone now for seven nights, four spent out in the open in the side tent. If all went well, he should be home tonight. As dawn broke he took down the side tent and rolled it up. He tied the kettle and mug onto the side of the pack-sack. Joe wondered what the going was like. He walked out on the pond for about a hundred feet. It was drifted hard enough to bear his weight and he figured he would make average time.

He came back to the fire and looked at the load he had to carry. He knew it would be tough going. His shoulders ached as he thought about strapping on the load. Joe said a prayer as he picked up the heavy pack-sack. He brought it up to his knees and put one arm through the sling. He clamped his teeth as he swung the load over his shoulders and quickly put his other arm through the other sling. As the weight of the load settled on his shoulders, he gave a loud yell and fell flat on his face in the snow. He lay there for a minute or two whimpering in pain. "Good grief," he whispered, "I'll never be able to carry it, my shoulders have had it."

But Joe Hancock, a man with the strength of an ox and a strong will, was not giving up. He summoned his courage and got to his knees. The straps of the pack-sack sank into his raw flesh and he felt a flash of blinding pain. He waited a minute as his vision cleared then slowly and painfully managed to get to his feet. Joe picked up the can of molasses and the other package and stepped out from the camp area. Tears came to his eyes with his first step, but he had to go on.

Crossing Clouds Pond wasn't bad due to the hard snow. However, when he took the trail through the forest the snow was deep and soft. He often sank but kept slowly moving on. It took him over two hours to get to Pinnacle Pond, a trip he would normally make in fifteen minutes. Pinnacle Pond was a mile long. Again, the snow drifts were hard and he made good time across. It would almost be impossible to relate what Joe suffered going from Pinnacle Pond to Devil's Cove Pond. He fell twice but somehow got to his feet and struggled on. He hoped to get to Beaver Cove by noon. If the ice was safe to cross Canada Bay at the narrows he should be home by late afternoon. The snow was getting soft as he left Devil's Cove Pond. He decided to take off his load and walk out and break the trail instead of tramping through the deep snow with the load on his back.

At noon, he reached Beaver Cove but he didn't stop to eat. He still had a little of the soaked hard bread left and decided to save it for a lunch late in the afternoon. When he came out on the salt water ice at Beaver Cove he noticed the center of the bay was all open water. The ice in the cove looked solid but as far as he could see around Beaver Cove Head it was open water. He got out on the bay. The going was much better. He would have to go along by the edge of Beaver Cove Head and trim the shoreline. The ice was broken up about a mile inside the narrows, but it was much better walking on the ice than in the woods so he kept walking at a fair pace.

Joe crossed the bay and headed out the left side. As he passed the narrows he found his snowshoes sinking into slob ice. This was not good. He would have to go ashore and keep close to the tree line. It was getting late in the afternoon. If he was to make it home before darkness set in he would have to continue at a faster pace. His left hand that gripped the molasses can was paining severely, but his fingers had no life in them. He stopped for a minute to switch hands and had trouble removing his fingers from the handle. He took off his frozen mitt and and examined his fingers. The tips were frozen and white. He rubbed his fingers in the snow and soon had life back in them. He put his mitt back on, took the molasses can in his right hand and walked on. When Joe reached the trail going across Bide Arm Neck he discovered snowshoe tracks. This was a welcome sight as he would have an easier time going the three miles to Bide Arm.

****

After Joe left Englee, Elizabeth and Fanny took turns keeping watch in the area near Glasberry Brook where Joe would come out on Bide Arm. After the fifth day they insisted that Mark or Roy go up the Arm to Glasberry Brook and walk across the trail to Canada Bay. They insisted the road should be kept open for Joe with his heavy load. They wanted his brothers to head across the Peninsula to meet him, but Skipper Jim wouldn't allow it. When the seventh day rolled around and there was no sign of Joe, the women became more concerned and decided to put pressure on the men.

"Aunt Fanny, tomorrow morning we will get ready and head in the Bay to see Eli Reid. He may know what happened to Joe," said Elizabeth.

"Yes, we'll wait one more day then we'll go. I know the way to the Tickles, all the way to Shoal Pond," said Aunt Fanny.

Elizabeth agreed, but looked continually up towards Bide Arm.

****

Joe kept going, staggering along like a drunken man. Hunger and pain were taking their toll. He didn't know how much further he could go without putting down the load and walking home without it. But no no, he thought, he would not leave the food no matter what. As Joe came along the trail he knew he would soon step out on the shoreline of Bide Arm.

****

Elizabeth Hancock melted the frost off the window and wiped it clear with a facecloth. She had the glass almost wiped away from staring up Bide Arm. The area around Glasberry Brook was in the shadow of the setting sun as she shaded her eyes and looked to see if Joe was anywhere in sight.

"Oh my,' she said as she strained her eyes. "I think I see something coming out on the ice. It's too big for a dog, might be a man. Yes, it looks like a man, could be Joe."

"What's that you said?" asked Fanny.

"I think I see something on the ice near Glasberry Brook," Elizabeth said in great excitement.

"What does it look like?" asked the anxious older woman.

"It looks like a man; it's in the shadow of the woods," said Elizabeth. "It must be Joe. Do you think it's Joe?"

"It's not much good for me to look, I can't see across the harbour. Call out to Roy and tell him to have a look," said Fanny.

Elizabeth went to the door and called out to Roy who was in the shed.

"What do you want?" he asked.

"Looks like someone just came out on the ice over near Glasberry Brook," said Elizabeth as she ran quickly back to the window.

Roy went up on the small hill not far from the house. He put his hand over his eyes to shade them and stared for a minute. He blinked his eyes and looked again.

"Looks like a man to me, it's either a man or a horse," he said as he called out to his father and Mark who were in the shed. "Come and have a look. Someone just came out on the Arm up near Glasberry Brook."

Jim Hancock was a tall and robust man and never known to get discouraged or downhearted. He came over to Roy and looked.

"Looks like a man to me," said Roy.

"It's a man all right," his father said.

"Do you think it's Joe?" asked Roy.

"There's only one way to find out. Get your snowshoes and you and Mark head out there immediately. I'll be behind you," said Jim. In less than two minutes the three of them were heading up Bide Arm.

****

Joe came out on the ice following the snowshoe tracks. His vision was blurred, but he knew the sun was setting from the reddish glow of the sun on the high hills across the east side of the Arm.

"I have another three more miles to walk, then I'll be home," he whispered. "I wonder if anyone is looking this way?"

Joe stopped and started waving even though he knew it was useless. He was in the shade of the woods and from Englee this area looked black. Joe later told his family that every step he took was like walking through the fires of hell. He stopped and put down the can and the package. He left his fingers in the hanger of the molasses can; if he removed them from the handle he might not get them through again. Then he leaned ahead and let the load rest on the center of his back, releasing some of the weight off the line straps. He started walking again. He figured he walked another half mile before stopping. It was beginning to get dark as he put down the load in his hands. He was staring at the snow when he heard someone say, "Joe, Joe is that you, Joe?" He straightened up and looked ahead. Two men were coming towards him, he couldn't recognize them.

"Joe, good Jingles, is that you?" asked a familiar voice.

Joe knew who it was. "It was me one time, but now I don't know," he said.

His two brothers grabbed him as he staggered and almost fell. Mark Hancock was known as the giant of Englee; some say he once lifted the main boom of a schooner, 1,800 pounds. And he was known to have killed six husky dogs with his fists when they attacked him one day while he was at Battle Harbour. That evening, when he caught Joe by the shoulder to prevent him from falling, he heard a sudden scream. "Good Jingles," he roared, "Wass rong?"

All Joe could say was, "The straps are cut into my shoulders, for God's sake take it easy." Joe wiggled his fingers out from the hanger of the molasses can and dropped the package, then straightened up and stared at his brothers. "Thank God you are here," he said.

"Take off the load," said Roy. "We'll take it."

"You have to be careful taking the straps from my shoulders. They are stuck in the flesh," said Joe.

Roy and Mark got on each side and took the weight of the load. Mark pulled one of the straps from a shoulder as Joe howled with pain. Mark told Roy to do the same. Roy hesitated.

"Hold this side," Mark yelled to Roy.

Roy switched to the other side. Mark quickly moved over and pulled the other strap off. Joe fell to the snow for a minute then got to his feet as if the world had been lifted off him.

"I thought I would never live to get this far. That was the worse load I've ever lugged," said Joe.

"Good grief, Joe, you mean to tell us you brought all of this from Flowers Cove?" asked Roy.

While they were talking their father arrived, almost running, and ready to give Joe a hug. "Don't touch him," roared Mark. "You could kill him outright Look at the blood on his sweater, the straps have cut right to the bone."

"Leave the hugs to Elizabeth," said Roy.

Jim Hancock couldn't believe Joe was in such rough shape.

"Did you get all the stuff we wanted?" asked Mark.

"Got it all," said Joe.

"Do you think you can walk home, Joe?" asked his father.

"I have to unless Mark carries me and the load," said Joe.

"Yes, jump up on the load, Joe," said Mark as he swung the pack-sack over his huge shoulders.

All the people around Heights Cove, the area of Englee where the Hancocks lived, came out of their houses to watch the mens' arrival. Aunt Fanny and Elizabeth went to the edge of the ice and watched as the men came closer. Elizabeth was happy to see Joe on his feet although at times he staggered. She ran to meet him. Mark said later Elizabeth thought Joe was returning from the Boer War by the way she kissed him. But before she put her arms around him he warned her not to touch his shoulders. It was then she saw the bloodstains on his sweater.

"My oh my, what in the world happened, Joe?" she asked.

"I'll tell you later, all I want to do now is sit down," he said.

Joe was escorted to the house and sat at the table. He was pale and cringing with pain. "The straps burst on the pack-sack. I had to use bank-line as straps, had no other choice, it cut the flesh to the bone," he explained.

Aunt Fanny, who was a midwife, took over. She told Joe to relax, that she would help him undress and see what damage he had done.

Joe knew his mother would fix him up.

Fanny and Elizabeth managed to get his clothes off, noting his underwear had strips of flesh stuck to it. Stanley Hancock, a relative of Joe's, said when telling this story that Aunt Fanny mixed fish salt with hot water and used it to soften the underwear to get it out of the deep cuts on Joe's shoulders. Joe yelled so loud that Mark wondered out loud if his mother was killing a pig in the kitchen. Fanny and Elizabeth bandaged Joe's shoulders. It took a long while for them to heal. He carried the marks to his grave.

****

When Jim Hancock unpacked the freight and discovered the white flour, raisins and baking powder, he was not a very happy man.

"You can't be trusted with money, Joe. You bought stuff you had no business to buy out of my money," he said.

"Mom wanted the white flour and raisins to make cakes for poor Charley," said Joe.

"Your mother didn't send you, I did," said his father.

Roy had enough education to figure things out and he

made up the cost of the items Joe bought at the Co-Op.

"Just a minute, Dad," he said. "Joe got the white flour and raisins free, according to his receipt and the change he brought back."

His father would never know it, but the raisin buns and steam puddings made from white flour and raisins for Sunday dinner was well worth the work of juggling the price of each item. That was a secret known only to Joe and to Albert Rose.

Sadly, Jim Hancock drowned at Bide Arm two years after Joe made the trip across the Peninsula.

The Lillian

I picked up Dr. Gillard at his home one spring morning and we drove to the back harbour of Englee to look at the heavy Arctic ice that was blocking Canada Bay. We sat watching a large iceberg and wondering where it had originated from.

While we talked we noticed an ice breaker slowly pushing its way through the ice heading into White Bay and that was when Doctor Gillard related the following story about the *Lillian* to me.

He started by saying he'd heard his father tell the story several times about the schooner from somewhere in Conception Bay, which came into Englee one spring on its way to Labrador to go fishing for the summer. This was, said Doctor Gillard, during the days before any schooners had engines; it was all sails back then.

CHAPTER
1

The crew of the fishing schooner *Lillian* from Bacon Cove in Conception Bay were very busy on this early morning in mid-May. Although the exact date is unknown it was probably around the turn of the century. It was after Dr.

Grenfell arrived in Newfoundland in 1892, because the midwife involved referred to Dr. Grenfell on the Labrador.

Peter Walsh of Bacon Cove was a very good fisherman. He fished in a schooner down on the Labrador for years before he was married. His father and grandfather fished before him. After Peter married he acquired his own schooner, and as his sons, Joseph (Joe) and Patrick (Paddy), grew to manhood they fished with him. The Walshes fished out of Batteau, Labrador with cod traps during the summer and trawled with long lines on the Grand Banks in the winter.

Peter knew what it was like to deal with the fish merchants through good times and bad. If you made a good voyage you squared your account with the merchant and probably had a little balance on the books for next spring when the time came to fit-out for the Labrador again. Every skipper fully understood before he took supplies from the merchant to go to Labrador that every effort had to be taken to have a full load of fish before returning home. The skipper knew too that his catch of fish had to be sold to the merchant supplying him. If not, the schooner would become the property of the supplier. Some skippers were of the understanding that even their house could become the property of the merchant.

In going to the Labrador, the schooner had to take aboard enough salt for a load of fish, enough food to feed the crew for at least three months, and arrangements had to be made with the merchant to supply the family left behind at home for three months. Cod traps, moorings, ropes, and extra canvas for a sail or two had to be taken on board. Sometimes a complete building had to be taken aboard in sections and then erected in the cove or inlet where the fishing took place. Getting ready to go down on the

Labrador was a very busy time for the Walshes. Neighbours gave them a hand loading their two cod-traps. They also towed a trap skiff, and had a sixteen-foot punt which they carried on deck.

This was a time when the crew went to haul the cod-traps they had to row their twenty-eight foot boat out through a raging sea where the undertow reached for you every minute. There was no weather forecast; no radio of any kind that told the weather in advance. The rain clothes worn were homemade, sewn from left over flour sack material soaked in linseed oil. When you sailed out of port, the deck compass was the only piece of navigational equipment aboard. Most of those fishing skippers didn't know there was any such thing as magnetic north and true north, it was just a course north. Ice conditions were a continuous nightmare and icebergs were especially feared. It seemed the bergs rolled over every cod-trap along the coast on purpose. Perhaps worst of all was that medical help was practically non-existent. Those were the conditions Skipper Peter Walsh and his crew faced as they got ready to head to the Labrador for the summer.

"I wonder what the weather is going to be like for the next few days?" Peter asked an old timer as he and his crew got ready to haul their punt aboard.

"Not bad for the next twenty-four hours, wind sou-west, but I'd say after that we're in for a few days of nor-east winds according to the ring around the moon last night."

"Have you heard anything about the ice?" Peter asked him.

"Someone reported a schooner came to Harbour Grace from up around Catalina. Said it was a solid jam of ice around there."

"According to that, with a fair breeze of sou-west wind, it could put us up around Catalina in a couple of days and keep the ice off," said Peter.

"If you get out of here tomorrow morning you could have a good run at it," said the old timer.

Peter had a meeting with his two sons and the shareman, Nicky White. "We are leaving at 5 a.m." Peter told them. "It looks like sou-west wind for a couple of days and if all goes well we should make Catalina before the ice blocks the bays."

Peter's wife had fifty loaves of bread baked and packed, along with molasses and pork buns by the dozens. Salt beef, pork and molasses were their luxuries. Hard bread in fifty pound burlap bags was the order of the day, accompanied by salt dried fish left over from the winter.

****

About a month before the *Lillian* cast off at Bacon Cove, Skipper Peter Walsh was complaining about a bad stomach and weakness. He drank bread soda in warm water and a treatment of steeped Bog-bean. (Bog-bean is a root that grows in small ponds around the barrens. It can be boiled up and steeped like a tea in order to help with a poor appetite.)

"You'll be all right, Peter, after you get the kinks worked out from being laid up all winter," his wife Alma said.

Peter laughed at that. He had built three boats during the winter and made a new cod-trap, all that besides cutting and hauling ten cords of firewood with two dogs. But although he didn't feel well, Peter felt it was nothing to get alarmed about. He had felt worse.

It was midnight and everything was aboard ready to go. At 5 a.m. Peter kissed his wife and said goodbye. Then the crew reefed the sails and the *Lillian* headed out the bay. The *Lillian* was a small locally built fishing schooner. She wasn't sheeted with green heart to withstand the bay ice, let alone to combat the ice floes that swept down from the Arctic regions during the winter. She had two masts that supported two sails with the steerage on deck in the open. Sleeping quarters and galley were at the front. Food supplies were stored at the rear of the vessel. All cooking was done by Joe, the oldest son.

The southwest wind started around midnight. The *Lillian* held steady as she leaned to the right into the breeze, however the wind picked up with the rising of the sun to about twenty-five knots per hour.

"We are going to have a good day if this keeps up. Should make pretty good progress by evening. We'll run till dark," said Peter.

In the distance to the northeast, Arctic ice was visible; Peter estimated it to be ten miles off. "If the ice keeps off and the wind stays like it is we should make Joe Batt's on Fogo Island by tomorrow night," he told the crew. This was good news. No one wanted to get caught in the ice or get ice bound in some cove for weeks with the fishing season starting.

Bacon Cove was close to eighty miles from Bay de Verde at the tip of Conception Bay. Peter said they should go into Bay de Verde for the night. He said to get around Baccalieu Island with this breeze of wind and especially after dark could be risky business. They all agreed.

After they arrived in Bay de Verde, Peter complained about pains in his back and stomach. Joe went ashore to a shop looking for something to ease his father's pains but he could find nothing.

"You could take him to see Nurse Barter. She'll check him and give him something for his stomach," said the store clerk.

Joe found the nurse's house and knocked. She told him to get his father. She said she would like to see him before giving him medicine. Joe thanked her and left. Peter Walsh refused to go ashore.

"I'm not going to see any nurse. I'll be all right in a couple of days. It's only the stomach flu," he said.

With the wind southwest, Bay de Verde harbour was like a pond and the *Lillian* and her crew spent a pleasant night there. Early the next morning the wind was still southwest. Before the rays of the sun appeared in the eastern sky the *Lillian* was on her way, heading through Baccalieu Tickle. Plenty of sailing skill was needed to maneuver the vessel along close by the towering cliffs. But the crew felt in safe hands. Peter Walsh was a seasoned sailor, he had been passing those cliffs every year from the time he was a boy of thirteen. He was now fifty-three.

The wind was fairly strong as they came through the tickle. In the early morning dawn Peter could see the faint light blinking on Green Island on the other side of the bay. He quickly took a course for Green Island. It was a hard day punching their way across Trinity Bay and Skipper Walsh stayed at the wheel. There were times when waves washed over the deck, but the *Lillian* kept her head high and moved slowly in a northwestward direction.

At 2 p.m. the schooner was off Green Island and headed for Cape Freels. Peter knew it would be too late to get around Cape Freels before dark so he decided he would run into Newtown, although he was in dread of the many shoals. He knew with the wind from the southwest it could be tricky getting in. Just before dark, and after a nerve-wracking experience, he got the vessel safely into Newtown. The schooner had been on the rough sea for fifteen hours.

Once the schooner was secured for the night, Pat started putting vegetables in the pot. With the sea so rough all day they couldn't even make tea and all they'd had to eat was buttered bread and water out on deck. Peter was still having pain. His sons wanted him to go ashore and look for something to ease it, but he insisted it was just gas that would pass away after a few days.

Early the next morning, the wind was changing.

"We are in for a southeast breeze," said Peter, after taking a look just before dawn.

"This is not a good place for southeast winds. We should get out of here while there's still a bit of wind from the southwest. We should at least get on the other side of Cape Freels," said Joe.

Peter agreed. "Get the anchor up and reef the sails," he said. "Once we get out of here we'll be okay."

They immediately pulled the anchor and hoisted the sails. In about half an hour they were out of Newtown and headed for Cape Freels, eight miles away. Around 10 a.m. the wind changed to the southeast as Peter had predicted. This was a fair wind, but a southeast wind was not good news to fishermen heading to the Labrador in their wooden schooners in the spring.

The greatest fear for fishermen was of a southeast wind that would drive the Arctic ice towards the shore, trapping all boats moving north. If that happened, a boat could be trapped in some cove or harbour for weeks on end, resulting in the crew missing the fishing season altogether. Because of that likelihood, every fishermen going north had to take great chances when dealing with wind and ice.

Captain Peter Walsh was determined not to get caught in this way. He wanted to get across White Bay before a gale of southeast wind came on and pushed the rough ice against the land. If he got across the bay he knew he have a better chance of geting free from a port or cove when the wind turned west and pushed the ice off.

They had fair wind after rounding Cape Freels. Far in the distance, about ten miles off, Peter could see the looming whiteness of Arctic ice with several towering icebergs glistening in the early morning sun.

"If all goes well and the wind stays the same, we should be close to Joe Batt's on Fogo Island before dark," he said.

"There's no sign of ice ahead to the northwest, Father," said Pat.

"There won't be any ice along this shore if the wind keeps this way. But it could block White Bay and that won't be good," said Peter.

"Tomorrow will tell the tale," said Joe. "If we get into Joe Batt's we'll get an ice report from someone there. There may be other schooners around."

Peter suspected the southeast wind would be on for a couple of days. Following this, it would usually blow back from the northwest.

"There is an old saying: a southeaster is always in debt to a northwester," said Peter.

"It's all right if it doesn't block this area. Northwest wind could jam the ice solid on the Horse Islands. If that happens, it could prevent us from going across White Bay," said Pat.

"All we can do is hope for the best the same as we've always done," said Peter.

During the afternoon the sea became very rough with

heavy rain. For a while it appeared they would go into the Wadham Islands. However, in the distance they could see Fogo Islands about ten miles away.

"We'll be better off if we keep going to Joe Batt's, it's a better harbour," said Joe. His father agreed and the *Lillian* proceeded to Joe Batt's, arriving there after dark.

During the evening, Joe and Nicky went ashore to one of the shops and asked about the ice conditions around White Bay. They were told there was a lot of ice in White Bay and around the Horse Islands. But they heard there wasn't any ice between Horse Islands and Grey Islands and all the way up to St Anthony. This was good news. After Joe related this information to his father it was decided to go on to Partridge Point or Cape St. John, then take a straight course for St. Anthony or even Cape Bauld, keeping well outside of the Horse Islands. Hopefully the wind would stay southeast for another day. By then, they would be well up to the Cape Bauld area.

The next morning the wind was still southeast with heavy sea. It was decided to wait a few hours before proceeding. The seas were too high to risk towing the trap skiff. Sometime around noon the wind slackened. The *Lillian* left port and headed for La Scie. It was a rough day, several times it was thought the trap boat would be lost. In the distance they could see Cape St. John. They kept going. Getting around Cape St. John was a harrowing experience. The little schooner was tossed every way possible. Peter had to be strapped to the wheel as seas rolled across the deck. and even the lashed down punt filled with water. As they came around Cape John in the late evening the wind increased to gale force. Peter gradually edged the *Lillian* into the shelter of White Bay. After he got out of the huge swells and into the shelter of the bay, he knew it would be impossible to get into Baie Verte because the wind was blowing out of the harbour so he decided he would have to run across the bay to Pacquet. He got into Pacquet after dark and anchored. It had been a very stressful day.

Peter Walsh was a very sick man. But he didn't want to tell his sons and Nicky, he felt as though he was dying from uncontrollable pain in his chest. Joe knew there was something seriously wrong with his father and wanted him to go ashore to see if anyone could give him something to ease the pain but he refused. Pat mixed bread soda and water in a glass and gave it to Peter.

"This may remove the gas in your stomach," he told him.

After Peter got the drink down he felt a little better.

"I'm sure you have gas, Father. We'll give you more of that stuff later and you'll be all right," Joe said.

"I think we should turn around and go back home. Father is really not well," said a worried Pat.

"I don't think we should turn around," Peter said as he looked sternly at his sons. "And I'll hear no more talk of that. I'll be all right in a couple of days."

Pat wasn't satisfied. It wasn't normal for his father to be like this. He kept insisting they return back home or take their father to someone who could give him medical attention.

"Listen to me, Pat," said Peter. "I think I am getting the flu. I should be better in a couple of days and, if I'm not, when we arrive in St. Anthony we'll try to see Dr. Grenfell. He has a small hospital there now. Last year when we saw him on the Labrador, he told us he had a hospital started in St. Anthony and one in Battle Harbour. I can go and see him."

"What about if you take real sick before we get there, what will we do?" asked Pat.

"We have to get to Labrador regardless. Someone has to pay the merchant for the supplies we have aboard and the food your mother has home to feed the rest of the family for the summer. If we don't get to Labrador we might as well all be dead. We'll lose everything we have, including this schooner, and I don't intend to lose her come hell or high water," said Peter.

"What about if you get too sick to get out of bed, what will we do then?" asked Pat.

"You know the way to Labrador. You've been going down there from the time you cut your first teeth. You know how to set the cod trap and where to put it in the berth, so don't go back home until you have a full load of fish."

"In other words, you're telling us not to turn around even if you're dying," said Joe.

Peter paused for a moment then firmly replied,"If I die, don't turn around, Joe. We have to get this schooner loaded with fish before it returns back home and that's that."

There was no further talk. They ate supper and crawled into their bunks.

CHAPTER
2

After daylight it was decided to pull up anchor, hoist one
sail, and move out the harbour with caution. Once they
were out of the harbour and could get a better view of the
ocean, Peter noticed that the wind was tripping from the
southwest. That was in their favour. The wind would
clear out White Bay and put the ice off shore, especially
if it happened to veer to the west. A decision was made
to keep close to the south side of White Bay unless a
clear view of open water was sighted which would then
allow them to go across the bay to the northwest side.
The *Lillian* had her canvas aloft. She was leaning to the
right as she swiftly moved with the southwest breeze,
hugging the shoreline as she passed through Horse
Islands Tickle.

Pat stood watch at the front, alert to every move and
listening to the sea splashing against the sides of the little
schooner. His mind wasn't on the voyage to Labrador,
though, he was thinking about his father and concerned
about how sick he was. He had never seen his father ill
before; the old man was as tough as nails. As Pat stood
worrying about his father, he saw an opening in the ice
straight ahead leading across White Bay.

"Dad," he called. "Looks like all clear water up ahead,
leading all the way across the bay. Come here and take a
look."

Peter called Nicky White to take the wheel, saying "Keep her steady as she goes." Peter then went to the front and took a look. He put up his hand to shade his eyes from the brightness of the glare from the ice. "You could be right, looks to be all open water," he said.

"Looks to be about a couple of miles wide. I wonder which way the tide is running?" said Pat.

"Running up for sure. This time of the year it's always that way," said Peter.

"What do you think? Should we make a run for them high hills over that way?" asked Pat.

"I'm not sure. The ice could close in pretty fast, but the wind is in the right direction to keep it open," said Peter.

He and Pat studied the opening, it appeared to be widening.

"I think we should make a run for it, them high cliffs across over there are in Hooping Harbour. If we could get across the bay from here it would save a full day's run, maybe more," said Peter.

"Well, let's make a run for it," said Pat.

"I'm not sure. It's getting late and I wouldn't want to get caught out there in the dark," said Peter.

"It won't be dark for another four hours and by that time we should be across," said Pat.

Peter didn't reply as he went back and took the wheel. In a couple of minutes he turned the *Lillian* to the right and headed for the opening leading across White Bay. After Pat saw his father pull the *Lillian* on the course across the bay he knew what had to be done. The trap boat had to be hauled closer to the schooner. They had it on a long tow line while sailing in open seas. But when going through ice or close to ice they usually shortened the tow line in order to prevent ice from getting between the trap boat and the schooner.

All was going well for roughly an hour then the sun broke through the clouds in the western sky. At once Peter knew what was going to happen. "We are going to have a west wind. Do you see that clearing in the western sky? It's going to haul the wind west as sure as you're aboard this boat," he told Pat and Nicky.

"What should we do?" Pat asked. He knew a west wind could cause the ice to come in on them and they could be stuck in heavy ice for some time.

"There's not too much we can do now only keep our fingers crossed. If the wind doesn't change for another hour we'll be out of the ice anyway," said Peter.

"I hope you're right," said Pat.

Minutes after they spoke the wind changed to the west and the ice started closing in on the *Lillian*. As the sun was sinking, the rough Arctic ice was closing in on both sides of the schooner.

Peter estimated they were approximately ten miles off the entrance to Hooping Harbour, and about one mile from the inside ice edge. There was no sea rolling; there was hardly any motion. The schooner sat silently in an ocean of ice that would occasionally crack as it slowly melted. There was nothing that could be done as far as moving the vessel. The *Lillian* and her crew were entirely at the mercy of the wind and tide.

The greatest fear was of being crushed. Everyone on the schooner knew there would probably be a couple of days of westerly wind, but they also knew they stood a good chance of not receiving too much damage from pressure caused by the west wind because they were away from the standing edge. All they could do now was wait.

****

Joe had fish and brewis cooked for late supper. Peter was the last one to come down to the forecastle and everyone wondered why he was delayed. As he came down through the companionway, Joe noticed something was not right. with his father.

"Is there anything wrong, Father?" he asked.

Peter didn't answer and Joe told him to sit down. Peter sat. He put his elbows on the table and put his hands to his face. He still didn't speak.

"Are you okay, Dad?" asked Joe.

It took a moment for him to reply. "I am not feeling well. I have a terrible pain in my chest and in my arm. I feel as if I am going to faint."

That did not sound very good. Pat was very concerned. He knew the symptoms of a heart attack. He'd heard people talk about them before. But his father couldn't be having a heart attack, could he?

"How long have you been like this?" Pat asked.

"For about ten minutes, the pain hasn't slacked at all."

"Joe, mix up a glass of bread soda in warm water. He might have gas," Pat said.

Joe quickly mixed up a glass of warm water with bread soda and gave it to his father. Peter drank the contents and tried to straighten up but groaned in pain instead.

"Why don't you lie down till supper gets on the table," said Pat.

Peter managed to lift himself and roll into his bunk.

"Just a minute, Skipper," said Nicky. "I'll pull off your rubbers."

"Thanks," said Peter as he tried to smile.

Nicky pulled the rubber boots off and helped Peter get his jacket off. Joe and Pat were worried when they saw Nicky helping their father remove his jacket. They knew this was something more serious than gas. The lamp over the table gave a faint glow around the forecastle, enough to see the agony on their father's face as he lay back in his bunk.

"Maybe you are faint from hunger. You haven't eaten anything since long before noon. We'll get your supper, you'll feel better then," said Joe, hoping against hope he was right.

"I don't want anything to eat yet, boys. I think this is more serious than hunger," said Peter.

Joe proceeded to get everything on the table for the evening meal. He keep glancing at his father as he groaned in pain. Pat got a cloth, soaked it in cold water and placed it on Peter's forehead saying it might do him some good. Peter lay there with his eyes closed and said nothing.

"Supper is ready boys," said Joe as he put the steaming hot pot of fish and brewis on the table.

Nicky and Pat started eating, they were hungry as they hadn't eaten since 10 a.m., but the thought of the skipper lying sick in the bunk next to the table made the meal tasteless. Joe joined in and ate his late supper.

While they were eating, Peter fell asleep and started to snore. It was unusual for him to snore while sleeping. No one had never heard him make a sound after he lay down. The three men looked at each other with surprised looks but said nothing. They thought it was better for Peter to be snoring in his sleep than to be awake and groaning in pain.

"Should we wake him?" whispered Pat.

Joe shook his head. "No, let him sleep for a few hours. He must be tired, he has been up since five this morning."

The three men finished their meal and cleaned the dishes and packed them away as they quietly talked about the ice and what could happen tomorrow if the wind changed. It was close to eleven when they decided to turn in. Peter had not moved. He lay in the same position, snoring heavily, with his face to the wall.

"I guess we should wake him and see if he wants something to eat. He should take his clothes off too," said Pat.

Joe agreed. It was at this point the three men got the shock of their lives. Pat gently called, "Dad, hey Dad," but his father did not reply.

Pat put his hand on Peter's shoulder and gently shook him.

"Dad, Dad, wake up and have something to eat." There was no response. " Good grief," Pat said.

Joe sprang to his feet and reached for the bunk where his father lay. "Dad, Dad, what's wrong with you? Wake up, can you hear me?" Joe was almost screaming. His father did not reply, just snored loudly.

Panic began to strike. The all realized something was very wrong with Peter. He was not responding. Joe moved the table to get closer to his father's bunk. He turned Peter over to get a look at his face and was frightened at what he saw. Peter had turned dark around the neck area and his eyes were glassy. Joe immediately realized his father was dying.

When Pat saw what was happening, he turned and ran up the companionway to the deck. He couldn't look at his father this way. In the meantime, Joe felt his father's pulse. It was very weak. Joe knew the end was near.

****

Peter Walsh was a very religious man. He supported the clergy and was involved in everything in the little village of Bacon Cove. His wife depended on him to provide a

living from fishing and to make decisions around the
house. Without him, she would have a hard time. As he
stood and sadly watched his father dying, Joe knew the
news of his father's death would destroy his mother. But
there was nothing Joe could do to revive his father or
stabilize him. Death was close and nothing could prevent
it. Pat came down into the forecastle; he was crying.

"Oh my, oh my, what are we going to do, Joe? If father
dies we are finished," he sobbed.

Joe knew Pat would feel even worse than him if their
father died because he was closer to him. "We have to
accept whatever is going to happen. I knew Dad was sick
all along," said Joe.

"But why didn't we turn around and go back home?"

"I wanted to, but the old man wouldn't agree to it, he
had one thing on his mind, fish," said Joe.

Just before midnight, Peter Walsh passed away.

****

After Peter Walsh died, Joe and Pat and Nicky went up
on deck. They were in a state of shock. The *Lillian* was
surrounded by heavy ice that gave off a bright glow in the
star lit night. Joe knew he would have to take a leading role
now that his father was dead. With a heavy heart he said
they would have to take Peter's body from the forecastle
where they ate and slept. The three men brought the body
up on deck, wrapped it in a sail, and put it aboard the punt.

"In the morning we will decide what to do from here
on," said Joe.

The three disheartened men returned to the forecastle,
still not believing what had just happened. Pat kept saying
he couldn't believe his father was dead, he just couldn't
believe it. Nicky White was speechless. Peter Walsh was

like a father to him. Nicky had grown up next door, almost lived in the Walsh home from the time he could walk. He knew Peter's death was going to hit the Walsh family hard. So many people depended on him, including his own family.

"If we weren't so far from home I would head back and forget about the Labrador," said Joe.

"My Lord, are you still thinking about going down on the Labrador?" asked Pat.

"You know what Dad told us a couple of days ago. Make sure we go to the Labrador and get a load of fish to pay for the supplies we got from the fish merchant. He said if we didn't, the merchant would take the schooner. I don't think we have any choice but to keep on going. We can be there in a couple of days once we we are freed from the ice," said Joe.

"But what are we going to do with Dad's body? We can't send it back home. There's nothing going that way," said Pat.

"We'll have to do something with it after we get free of the ice," said Joe.

"If we are going on to Labrador there's only one thing we can do. We'll have to go in somewhere and bury him. In the fall when we return, we'll pick him up and carry him home," said Pat.

Joe agreed, thinking it was the only thing they could do. Pat started to cry. He couldn't take it any more. His father's death had broken his heart.

****

As the dawn lit up the eastern sky it was obvious weather was coming. Joe estimated they were about twelve miles off land and about a mile into the ice from the standing edge. They knew if the wind came from any point between east and southwest it would loosen the ice around them and this would give them fair wind to get to some community on the eastern side of the Northern Peninsula. It was a long morning waiting to see what was going to happen. The three men did a survey of the land northwest of their position and agreed it was the opening of Canada Bay.

"There's a town on the east side of the bay called Englee. We went in there out of a storm a couple of years ago. If the wind comes in on the land, we'll make a run for Englee," said Joe.

Pat agreed, but he couldn't bear the thought of leaving his father's body in some strange place for the sake of going to the Labrador to get a load of fish.

"How are we going to notify Mom?" Pat asked.

"We'll ask the clergy to write a letter and tell her what happened, and say that we'll bring his body home in the fall," said Joe.

The morning wore on till noon. Then the wind pitched from the southeast. Minutes after the wind struck, the ice started to slacken around them and a lead opened up towards the land. The three men immediately hoisted the canvas and the *Lillian* leaped into the wind, heading for Englee.

CHAPTER
3

Jessie Hopkins of Englee was a young midwife who had trained under the supervision of Dr. Wilfred Grenfell in St Anthony around 1898-98, according to Emma Canning-Fillier, who trained with her.

Jessie was the daughter of William Hopkins who kept the church in Englee. For years, William christened, married and buried everyone who needed the service. It was said he once buried a man who was alive but was supposed to have drowned. William was in his fish stage mending salmon nets when someone said a schooner was coming in the harbour. Stopping his work, William walked to the window and looked out and, sure enough, a schooner with a trap boat in tow was making her final cut before lowering her sails.

"Looks like a Labrador schooner. Can you make out the name, my eyes are bad?" he asked his son. Young Bill had been holding up the twine his father was using to repair his nets. The boy walked to the window.

"I can't make it out, but I think it starts with an L," he said.

William put down his needle and pushed across the sliding door. He peered out. He asked Bill, who now had a clearer view, to spell out the letters. Young Bill shaded his eyes and said, *"L-i-l-l-i-a-n."*

"It's *Lillian*, it's the *Lillian*, she must be on her way to

the Labrador," said William. He and his son watched the
schooner as it smartly turned into the wind. Her speed was
enough to make the Norris company wharf on the other
side of the harbour and throw ashore a line. In less than
five minutes, the *Lillian* was tied up. William watched the
schooner for a few minutes more and was surprised to see
the people aboard hoist the Union Jack flag to half-mast.

"There's something wrong aboard that schooner," he
said. "They hoisted their flag only halfways up and that
means there's something wrong aboard. I'm going across
the harbour and see what's up. You come with me."

Accompanied by his ten-year-old son, William quickly
rowed the three hundred yards across the harbour and
stopped near the side of the *Lillian*.

"Hello. Hello," he called.

Nicky White heard him and responded.

"I see your flag is at half-mast. Is there something
wrong?" William asked.

"Yes sir, there is something wrong" said Nicky. "I'll get
Joe and he can tell you about it."

In a minute or so Joe came to the railing and looked at
the bearded man and boy in the punt. At first, he didn't feel
like telling them about the death of his father, but someone
had to know. "Our father died yesterday evening. We have
him aboard," he stammered.

"I'm very sorry to hear that sad news. May I come
aboard?" William asked.

Joe sensed something in the man's voice and invited
him aboard. William climbed aboard, noting the sorrow on
the faces of the three men.

"Our father died around midnight last night," said Joe.

"Had he been sick very long?" asked William.

"No, just a few complaints here and there. He said he

had a bad stomach and we thought it was gas or some minor thing," said Pat.

"Sometimes it doesn't take much to cause a man's death," said William.

"Dad was different. He was tough as nails, never had an ache nor pain in his life, but in a couple of hours he was gone," said Joe.

"Is there a clergyman here, sir," asked Pat.

"No, there's no clergy here as such. I am the lay reader for the Methodist congregation. If there's anything I can do for you men I will gladly do it," said William.

"We would like to talk to you, sir," said Joe.

William held out his hand. "I'm William Hopkins," he said. "And this is my son Bill."

"I'm Joe Walsh. This is my brother Pat and our shareman, Nicky White. Our father is Peter and we are from Bacon Cove, Conception Bay."

William shook hands with the three men.

"We are on our way to Batteau, Labrador. A couple of days ago Dad felt sick and the last thing on our minds was that he was going to die. But he told us if he died we had to continue to the Labrador. He said if didn't the fish merchants would take our schooner and everything else we have, so I guess we have no other choice but to proceed on to the Labrador," said Joe.

By now other people was gathering on the wharf after seeing the flag flying at half-mast. Joe very quietly asked William to come to the forecastle to talk privately. There, he and Pat discussed what they wanted done with their father's body.

"We wondered if it was legal for us to bury Dad here at Englee, then in the fall when we are returning back home we can dig him up and take his body with us?" asked Joe.

"I don't know. I have never heard of that being done, but I suppose it can be. I've never seen any law against it," said William.

"I have heard of it," said Pat. "Several people died while fishing down on the Labrador and they were buried and dug up and brought home on the return voyage."

"If that's the case, and if it's what you want, then we'll gladly do it," said William. "When do you want to hold the funeral?"

"Well, we're in sort of a jam," said Joe. "A solid field of ice is heading this way. We're afraid we are going to get ice bound here and be stuck for some time. So we were wondering if we could hand Dad's body over to you and you could bury it for us and mark the grave. If you can do that, we can move on and get ahead of the ice."

"That's no problem. We can take care of everything. Just give us the proper information about your father, his age, the next of kin, the cause of death and the date he died. We should be able to do the rest," said William.

"Whatever charge there is, we will pay you in the fall when we return," said Pat.

"That's fine," said William and then added, "My daughter is a trained midwife. She will be able to dress the body and prepare it for burial."

"Okay, Mr. Hopkins, we will hand Dad's body over to you and be on our way," said Joe.

"There's one more piece of information I'll need. What's his religion?" asked William.

"The old man didn't belong to any religion and we are the same," said Joe.

"In that case, if it's legal, I'll put him in the Methodist cemetery until you return," said William. Joe and Pat agreed. William took his carpenter's pencil and scratched down as best he could the necessary information about Peter Walsh that he would need for the death certificate. William didn't show it but he was surprised the boys didn't want to have a funeral for their father before they left for Labrador. It was obvious to William Hopkins that fishing was more important than the burial of their father. Nothing else was discussed.

William and the two Walsh brothers went back on deck. There were now about twenty men gathered on the wharf, all curious about the flag at half-mast. Nicky told the men about the death of Peter Walsh. Joe led William to the punt containing his father's body.

"We have him rolled up in a piece of canvas. We had no lumber to make a casket," he said.

"We will take care of everything. It is our duty to be of service to you," said William. Joe and Pat thanked him.

A group of men came aboard and lifted Peter Walsh's body from the punt and handed it to others on the wharf. Businessman Bernard Norris heard the commotion and came and talked to Joe, who told Norris the situation they were in and about the field of ice coming this way.

"We are forced to move on. If we don't get to Batteau on time our trap berth will be taken and that means our summer fishing will be lost. Every hour counts now."

"You're right, young man" said Norris. Being a fish merchant, Bernard Norris understood full well what the crew was talking about and his opinion was that they were responsible men. "If all the fishermen around here were as dedicated as these three we'd have tons of fish by now," he told William after the *Lillian* left port. William didn't comment.

William told the men to get a hand-barrow and take Skipper Walsh's body across the harbour and have it put in his store loft. He said he would have the midwife dress it and prepare it for burial. After the body was on its way to the store loft and things settled down aboard the *Lillian*, Bernard Norris told the crew who he was.

"You don't have to worry about the cost of anything," Norris told them. "If there's any cost I will take care of it. I'm the merchant here."

"Thanks, Mr. Norris. We wish the fish merchant out our way was as kind and considerate as you. If he was, we wouldn't have to worry about anything," said Pat.

"What time do you expect to be back?" asked Norris.

"Maybe mid-August or whenever we get a load of fish. We are hoping to have at least twelve hundred quintals," said Joe.

"If you're interested, when you come in to get your father's body, I will pay you cash for your load of fish," said Norris.

Joe Walsh had never seen cash paid for fish. Norris's offer was too good to refuse. "We will think about it during the summer," he said.

Bernard Norris was a shrewd operator. He had a buyer for the fish and he knew that by paying cash he would get a good deal. As for the Walsh brothers, a cash payment meant they would end up with more than enough money to pay off the merchant in Bacon Cove and still have some to put in their pockets. After their conversation, the sails were hoisted and the *Lillian* moved out, leaving the skipper's body in the hands of strangers.

CHAPTER
4

William Hopkins rowed back across the harbour, figuring he had seen it all. Just as he reached his stage head he saw the *Lillian* hoist her sails and head out the bight.

"I don't think those boys respect their father. I know that I wouldn't do what they are doing to my father," he said to his son as he got ready to climb onto his wharf.

William knew it would take a while for the men to bring Peter's Walsh's body around the harbour to his store loft. Knowing he had some time he asked young Bill to go get his sister Jessie.

"You have a task to take care of in a few minutes," William told his daughter when she arrived and asked why he wanted her.

Jessie looked at her father and could tell he was troubled.

"What is it, Father?" she asked.

"Did you see the schooner that just left?"

"Yes, I also saw it when it came in about an hour ago. Why? "

"The skipper of that schooner passed away yesterday. The sons came in and left his body with us. They want it buried temporarily until they return from the Labrador. Then they want us to dig up the remains, put them aboard their vessel, and they will take them back home for the burial in their hometown," he told her.

"Good Lord, Dad, are you serious?" she asked.

"Yes, that's what they wanted," he replied.

"I doubt if that can be done without special permission from the government," she said.

William stared at his daughter with a puzzled look. Maybe he had accepted a task he couldn't do. "What part of the burial could cause a problem?" he asked.

"The part where we dig up the corpse again," said Jessie.

William was a bit put out. But it was too late now. The *Lillian* had left port and he had a dead man on his hands who would have to be buried by tomorrow. Someone would have to come up with a solution as soon as possible. "We are going to have to send for Louie. She may know what to do to get us out of this jam," he said.

Just then some men arrived with the body, followed by about thirty others.

"Bring him in the stage and place him on the splitting table. It's cooler down there," William told them.

Louie arrived on the scene in about half an hour. Louisa Canning was an older Grenfell-trained midwife, a heavyset woman, very stern and distinguished looking.

"What's going on?" she asked Jessie.

"Dad can explain it better than me. He was involved from the beginning," said Jessie.

Louie held up her hand for William to be silent, then told the crowd to leave. "Now William," she said after everyone was gone. "Tell us what's going on. Is it true you have a body, the real body of a man there in the splitting stage?"

"Yes, Louie. We do have a body. The man's name is Peter, just a moment...." William took out a piece of wrinkled paper. "Here it is, his name is Peter Walsh, he is fifty-three years old, from Bacon Cove, and he died last night around midnight."

"Do you know the cause of death?" she asked.

"No, his sons said he was never sick in his life. He had a few pains for a few days, but except for that he was a healthy man."

"I see," she said.

"They wanted him buried right away."

"Is there anything else they told you about what happened?"

"No, only that they want him dug up again sometime in August when they return so they can take him back home to be buried."

Louie thought for a few moments then replied, "That is impossible. You can't bury a man for a couple of months then dig him up and transplant him somewhere else without the government giving their okay and that is usually a long process. On the other hand, William, how do we know the man wasn't murdered?"

The thought had never entered his mind and William didn't know how to answer. "What should we do?" he asked.

"There's only one thing for us to do now. Perform an autopsy on the body. We can tell if he died of natural causes or if someone killed him," said Louie.

"How in God's name would you do that?" he asked.

"I assisted with a couple of autopsies while training in St. Anthony. I guess Jessie and I can do one on the skipper," she said.

"Are you allowed to do it?" he asked.

"Yes, I have a license for such work," she said.

William shuddered at the thought of cutting up a

human body. "I believe his sons said their father died from pains in his chest and stomach. We should leave it at that and bury him," he said.

"When the time comes to bury him, Uncle William, you will do your job, sing a hymn, read the burial and offer up a prayer and we won't interfere. But before that happens, we have to find the cause of death to fill out the necessary papers. We don't expect you or anyone else to interfere with us," said a stern Louie Canning. "Now, I want to have a short conversation with Jessie. You men run along." Louie looked at Jessie, "Have you ever seen an autopsy preformed?" she asked.

"No," said Jessie.

"It's no different than the birth of a child except it could be a little messier," said Louie. " You just heard me saying we won't be allowed to bury the skipper and have him dug up again in a couple of months unless we obtain special permission from the government. So, what we will do is fill him with fish salt after we remove his stomach. Then we'll put him in a coffin and salt him away. We can store him in a safe place till his sons return from the Labrador."

Louie told William to have a couple of men build a casket. He guaranteed a strong one would be built.

"We won't began the work until after dark, because people are always snooping around. We'll start the work at ten tonight. I have a good lantern and the tools to perform the autopsy," said Louie.

"Maybe we should have Elizabeth assist us. It will be a good experience for her," said Jessie.

Louie agreed and told Jessie to talk to Elizabeth.

****

At this point in the story, Dr. Gillard and I decided to

stop in somewhere and have a cup of tea. While we were drinking it he told me about his mother, the 'Elizabeth' Louie and Jessie were talking about. "Mother was one of the girls who went to St. Anthony hospital and trained with Louie and Jessie. That was before she married. Dr. Grenfell insisted that women should receive training for delivering babies. These women did great work and I suppose few of them ever received a penny." That said, we nodded in agreement and Dr. Gillard continued his story.

****

That night, when Louie, Jessie and Elizabeth gathered to perform the autopsy, it was dark and quiet. The only sound was the lonely howl of a dog penned up somewhere. The three midwives carried a kerosene oil lantern as they walked down to the wharf. Earlier in the evening they had talked about how they would check to find the cause of death. Louie said if they suspected any foul play they would contact the proper authorities immediately. By mail, of course, and that would probably take months.

The midwives had no rubber gloves, but Elizabeth carried a pint jar filled with Jeyes Fluid, which they would use to disinfect their hands before handling the body. The splitting stage where they would do their work was not completely sealed. It had been built using green lumber and the hot sun dried the lumber causing large seams to open up. When the midwives' bright lantern was lit inside, nosy people outside could see a lot of what was taking place inside. Louie knew people were watching, but she wasn't concerned. The work could and would still be done.

The midwives cut Peter Walsh's clothes off. Louie said all they had to do was cut his stomach from the chest bone down and then pull the stomach out. The women saw no signs of bruising or fractures around the head or any other part of the body. They examined Peter's lungs and saw no problem. But when they sliced into his heart they had no doubt he'd died of a heart attack. Louie said they would put the stomach and lungs in a sack and have William bury it. She then ordered Jessie to go tell her father they were ready for the casket.

When Jessie stepped outside the stage door she saw the casket on the wharf. It had rope handles along the sides. Four or five men were standing not far from the stage and she asked them to help salt away the body. Everyone refused, except for Edger Barnes and Levi Canning. They came and helped fill the body of Skipper Peter Walsh with coarse fish salt. After the women sewed up the body, they placed it in the casket and Louie wrapped a linen cloth around it, whispering a short prayer as she did so. The casket was quickly filled with salt, nailed closed, and placed in the ceiling of William's store loft. Louie filled in the necessary papers and sent them to the government. She didn't get a reply.

During the summer, several people said they saw the ghost of a man walking near William's stage. That resulted in no one walking the roads after dark in Englee as long as the schooner captain rested in the loft of William's storeroom.

Sometime during the middle of August, the *Lillian*, fully loaded with salted fish, came into Englee and tied up at the Norris wharf. Joe immediately went to the office of Bernard Norris where he agreed to sell him his load of fish. Joe then asked to see William and was taken to his home on the other side of the harbour. Sitting over a cup of tea, William explained everything that had taken place. He told about the autopsy and how it was against the law to remove a body without special permission from the government.

"So we didn't bury your father," he finished up. "We placed him in a casket and salted him away. He's in the top loft of my store. Has been there all summer."

Joe was pleased with the news. "I guess it's better to take home a salted body than one half rotten," he said.

"When we get the casket for you we'll empty out the salt to lighten it," said William.

"There's lots of time," said Joe. "We will be here for two or three days as we are selling our load of fish to Bernard Norris. After that, we will take our father's remains and be on our way."

Three days later, the *Lillian* slipped out of Englee with the body of Captain Peter Walsh lying in a casket in the ship's hold. The people in Englee never heard from anyone aboard again.

During the fall, Dr Grenfell came to Englee on his way to St. John's. He was told about this incident and said he would have done the same thing if he'd been there. He told the midwives they had done a great job.

****

Dr. Gillard laughed as he sat back in his chair. "I'd say," he said, "if there had been a hole through Peter Walsh the size of a baseball they would still have said he died of a heart attack. It was after that Mother got married to Noah Gillard and I am the result."

The Matchmaker

CHAPTER
1

The wind was off to the west, blowing the fourteen-foot punt sideways. The two young boys rowing the punt had to work hard battling the six-foot waves as they rounded the massive headland that rose straight from the water.

"Don't keep her off too far from the shore in this breeze of wind or we'll capsize," said Liddy Newman, who was manning a sculling oar in the back of the punt. The boys rowing were her sons, John, fourteen, and Elijah, thirteen.

"We can't do any more, Mom. You'll have to steer her yourself," said John.

Thirty-eight-year-old Liddy had arms like an ox. With seemingly little effort, she quickly turned the punt towards the granite cliff, moving her sculling oar with great speed.

"We have to keep her inside Granfers Rock even if she goes to the bottom," she told the boys. "If we go outside the rock we'll be too far out into the wind."

"I don't think we'll be able to row her into the wind, Mom," said Elijah. "Looks like the sea is too high, it's breaking right to the shoreline."

****

Lydia Randell Newman became a widow at age thirty-six when Eli, her forty-year-old husband, died after going through the ice and developing pneumonia in both lungs. Eli's unexpected and tragic death left Lydia with eight children, ranging in age from six months to fourteen years, no money, no fishing equipment and few supplies.

Eli had fished with Tom Randell and his crew from Little Harbour Deep, three miles away. When he was fishing, Eli would be gone for several days at a time especially when the weather was blustery and the winds were high. He made a living fishing during the summer and sawing lumber with a pit-saw during the winter. Eli was a good provider. His children always said they never saw a day when there wasn't food on the table.

Eli had large fish flakes near his house at Granfers Cove. After he brought home his share of salt shore fish he would wash and dry it. It was Liddy's job to tend the flakes while the fish was drying. Once it was dry, it was sold to the fish merchant but there was no money exchanged, just turn in the dry fish for food and supplies. Besides helping with the fish, Liddy tended the small vegetable gardens near the house. The family depended on the vegetables she grew to get them through the winter.

Eli had used his fourteen-foot punt to go back and forth from Granfers Cove to Little Harbour Deep. Sometimes, when the west or northwest winds were too high, he would walk over the mountains, a distance of some five miles. After Eli's death, life changed drastically for Liddy. Now she was the sole breadwinner with help from her two teenage sons.

A few days after Eli's funeral, Skipper Tom came to Granfers Cove and met with Liddy. Tom was a war veteran whose jaw had been partly shot off overseas leaving him with a speech impediment. Knowing Liddy was in desperate straits, Tom offered her a berth fishing in Eli's place.

"You won't have to go out in the boat to haul the cod-traps," he said. "I'll give you a job in the fish-stage salting fish, which is what Eli did. Your two oldest boys can work at the fish as well. Between the three of you you'll get a full share."

Liddy was very pleased with Tom's offer and realized she would be able to get at least half a living with the fishing. She knew, however, she wouldn't be able to tackle a pit-saw during the winter months, but somehow, no matter what, she would try to keep the family fed.

She thanked God her oldest child was a girl. Without her daughter's help, she would never have been able to leave home every morning and try and earn a bite to eat. Liddy was well aware that what she was doing could lead to problems. Here she was leaving her five youngest children, including the six-month-old baby, in the care of her twelve-year-old daughter.

Every morning, Liddy rose from her bed at dawn. She made breakfast for the two boys who were going with her, breast-feed the baby, and then put the baby in bed with her daughter. With that done, she and her sons headed for Little Harbour Deep by way of the Labrador Sea, the cruelest waterway in the world. Day after day the hard-working mother and her sons battled wind and tide, as well as rain, drizzle and fog and, some mornings, even snow flurries.

It was a grueling summer for Liddy. Her hands were calloused from sculling and rowing the punt. Her arms were literally burnt from using so much rock salt making the fish. At one point, she suffered from huge boils on her arms. So called water pups, the boils or sores are common among fishermen whose skin is often in contact with salt water. But nothing at all deterred Liddy. She was a go-getter. Tom Randell often said, "If I wasn't married to a good woman I would marry Liddy right away. That woman is worth her weight in gold."

Liddy and her sons didn't miss a day of work at Little Harbour Deep. If there was fish to be salted they were there, either in the punt or walking overland in bad weather. However, when everything got tallied in August, Liddy realized what she and her sons had made would only get the family enough food to last half the winter. And there was no way she could get her mind around the idea of tackling the pit-saw in January. Liddy didn't know what she was going to do, but she vowed she would do anything before she would let her family starve.

And now, Liddy was deep in thought as the little punt bobbed and tossed in the undertow as it squeezed along the shoreline in the breaking sea. She manned the sculling oar as her sons rowed with all their strength. "We made it through," she yelled above the roaring of the mighty Atlantic. Elijah gave his mother a faint smile, indicating he had heard her. The three souls manning the oars slowly pulled the raggedy little punt into the fishing village of Little Harbour Deep. Yet again, they had won another battle in the fight for existence.

****

Thomas Ellsworth was from Betts Cove on the Baie Verte Peninsula. Early one stormy morning, a fishing schooner heaved to off the back harbour near Englee. Someone was put in a small dory and the schooner sailed away with no one giving a backward glance. The person sent ashore was Thomas, a good looking young man of seventeen, six feet two inches tall with broad shoulders.

He rowed to a fishing wharf and came ashore. Seeing a large house not far from the wharf with smoke coming from the stove pipe, he knew someone must be up so he went to the door and knocked twice. The door was opened by an unpleasant looking man wearing heavy trousers held up by suspenders and with an obvious mouthful of chewing tobacco. Thomas said hello twice without getting a reply. The man finally stepped close to the threshold and let go a squirt of tobacco juice that almost hit Thomas's ear.

Thomas didn't move as the man turned without speaking and walked back into the house. Thomas stood and stared at him for a moment, wondering what was going to happen. The man finally turned and looked at him. "Well, get in here and shut the door," he growled. "I'm George Compton and I'm not as bad as the ones who just tossed you off that schooner, but I'm not the holiest man in the world either. I wouldn't hesitate to cut your throat if I didn't like ya."

Thomas entered the house and closed the door. George Compton's talk didn't frighten him. Thomas had worked on schooners since he was twelve and had fought many times with the toughest on board. Following George to the kitchen, he sat on a stool near the stove. He could smell fish cooking and noticed a large plate of sliced bread in the center of the table. George walked to the washstand in the corner where he poured water from a pot and washed his face. He then went to the bottom of the stairs and yelled, "Get up or I'll come and beat up the bunks."

The table was laid for four people. George went to the dresser and added another place setting. Thomas wondered when the older man was going to ask him about himself, but he said nothing. George was silent as he lifted the steaming boiler from the stove and went outside and drained off the water. Coming back in, he took out the fish and put it on the table.

"Pull up the bench and get your part before the gang arrives," he said. Thomas obediently reached for a piece of fish. "One second," said George. "You'd better say grace."

"Say grace, what's that?" asked Thomas.

"Just what I figured. I knew you were a heathen when I opened the door, but at least you speak English," said George as he followed up with a short blessing and told Thomas to dig in.

George Compton's three sons were surprised to see a stranger sitting at the breakfast table.

"Who are you?" asked Art.

"I'm Thomas Ellsworth."

"When did you arrive, and how did you get here?" asked Dorman.

"I'm from a Canadian banking schooner that was fishing fifteen miles southeast of the Grey Islands. We came into Grey Islands for fresh water last night and a fight broke out. The captain accused me of starting it. We were on our way to Conche for bait when he decided to throw me ashore. That's how I came here," said Thomas.

"What are you going to do now?" asked Art.

"I don't know. Maybe you fellows can give me a job. I know all about fishing. I also know everything about sailing. I was in charge of sailing aboard the banker."

"We don't need any more men," said George. "I got three who are too lazy to get out of the bunk. I don't need you. But there might be someone around here who needs another man."

"I'll work for nothing, just my grub," said Thomas.

"That's what the dogs do, work for their grub," said George.

"I'm prepared to do whatever I can until I get a passage back home or get a job somewhere," said Thomas.

"Okay young fellow, you can be my dog until you get a passage out of here or get a job somewhere," George told him.

Jack Newman, aged ninety-three, is a grandson of Liddy Newman, and he says Thomas Ellsworth was a dog to old George Compton and worked for him for just his food for more than a year. Jack said Thomas was a likable fellow, a hard worker, and all the women loved him.

After deciding to stay on in Englee, Thomas eventually ended up as a fish culler and buyer for David Norris, the local fish merchant. He was also an expert at operating the company's sailing vessel, which is what brings him into this story about the Newmans and Reids of Canada Bay.

When Thomas was twenty he got married. At that time he left the employ of David Norris, built his own trap skiff and went fishing on his own. However, it didn't work out and it wasn't long before he went back collecting fish for Norris.

CHAPTER
2

Thomas meets the widow

The trap fishing season was almost over, the fish had left the shoal water and went off-shore to the banks.

Thomas Randell took his traps from the water, cleaned them, and stored them away for another season. His job now was drying the salt fish and preparing it for market. Thomas did for Liddy as he had done for Eli. He weighed out her share of cod, carried it to Granfers Cove and helped stack it in the fish store on her wharf. With the help of her two sons and some of her neighbors, Liddy washed the fish and dried it in the sun. In less than two weeks the fish was ready for market.

Thomas Ellsworth had never met Liddy Newman. But then he was sent to the Little Harbour Deep area to collect fish. It was Tom Randell who told him about Liddy, what a tremendous woman she was and how daring she was in battling the rough weather to get to work. Tom said Liddy was going to have a rough winter. He said the fish she had would only give her enough food supplies for half the winter and he noted she had eight children, a lot of mouths to feed. Thomas Ellsworth would be going to Granfers Cove the following day to collect fish. He would meet Liddy then.

Liddy had fifty quintals (one quintal equals 112 pounds) of fish. With the grade of fish she had she knew there should be a return of one hundred and twenty-five dollars, an average of two dollars and twenty-five cents per quintal. There was no doubt about it, the amount of money coming to her would not buy enough food for the winter. She couldn't sleep at night wondering what to do.

Thomas Ellsworth sailed into Granfers Cove and let down the anchor. He sounded the whistle three times, signaling he was here to take fish. Thomas was anxious to see Liddy Newman. He was curious about this tough old lady he'd heard so much about.

Thomas had two men with him. He knew he had about an hour before the people of Granfers Cove would be ready to bring their fish to the schooner so he decided to go ashore and inspect the fish in the different sheds. He landed at a wharf where people were busy loading their fish into their trap skiff. After inspecting the fish, he asked someone where Liddy Newman lived. The next stage over, he was told.

Thomas went to the stage and saw a group of people carrying fish to the front of the wharf and loading it aboard their small rickety punt. He noticed a fair looking woman with big hands packing fish in the wheelbarrow. He figured she was around thirty, not much older than his wife.

"Is Mrs. Liddy Newman around?" he asked her.

"Yes, sir, I'm Liddy Newman. You must be the fish buyer Thomas Ellsworth," she politely said.

Looking surprised, he said he was.

"We only have a small punt but we should be able to put our fish aboard your schooner in four or five trips," she said.

"So you're Liddy," he said with a grin. "I was expecting

to see an old lady wearing a shawl and ready to take on the world."

Liddy laughed, "Don't believe all the lies you hear. Some people will tell you anything."

Thomas looked at her. She was a very noble looking person. If he wasn't married he would be calling on her.

"Will you be anchored at Granfers Cove for the night?" she asked.

"Yes, until noon tomorrow," he replied.

"You can have supper with us if you want," she said.

"I accept the invitation," he said.

At five-thirty, Thomas sat at Liddy's table with her eight children. He enjoyed a lovely meal of fresh garden vegetables, prepared by Liddy's twelve-year-old daughter.

After supper, Liddy talked about her fear of not being able to provide for her children over the winter. She said it would be impossible for her to go to a logging camp and stay with a bunch of men and saw logs with a pit-saw like Eli in order to keep food on the table. She said she just wouldn't be able to do it.

"Isn't there anything else you can do to make a living?" Thomas asked.

"Not here in Granfers Cove," she said.

"I heard there was an orphanage started by Dr. Grenfell, an Englishman, at St. Anthony. Maybe you could go there."

Liddy thought for a few moments. "If there was no other hope then I guess I would have no other choice," she said.

"After meeting you, I can tell you're not going to sit around and wait until the last loaf of bread is on the table, are you?"

"No, I'm not. I'll make up my mind about what to do

before the last mail boat stops running in November."

"Are you interested in getting married again?"

"If I could get a good man, someone who would look after me and my eight children, I would consider it," she said after a moment's pause.

"You're still a young woman," Thomas smiled.

"I turned thirty-nine two weeks ago. I'm not old, but I have eight children and what man in his right mind would take me on. He'd have to be a millionaire," she said with a laugh.

Around 9 p.m. one of the men with Thomas came to bring him back to the schooner. Thomas said many times afterwards he had a restless night thinking about Liddy Newman, and wondering how she was going to make it through the winter with her eight children. There was no doubt about it. He would have to find a man for her, but who?

The next morning, with the fish all collected, Thomas delivered goods to the wharf where Liddy and her sons waited, he even gave her a little extra and said it had been very nice having supper with her and her family.

She thanked him for the comment. Thomas then said he would like a private word with her. She invited him back to her house where he told her he was troubled about how she was going to cope in the coming winter. "You said if you could find a good man who would take care of you and your children you would consider marrying," he said.

"Yes, I would consider it," she said.

"I know of a good man who is very well to do. He would take care of you and your children. His wife died recently and he may be interested in marrying again."

Liddy was silent. She didn't have the faintest idea who he was referring to.

"The man I am talking about is a close friend of Mr. Norris, the fish merchant, and also a close friend of Dr. Grenfell, the English doctor in St. Anthony."

"Where does this man live?"

"He lives up in Canada Bay, on Old House Point. He has a farm where he grows vegetables and raises cattle for the Grenfell Mission. His name is George Reid and he is forty-four years old."

Liddy had heard of George. He sold vegetables along the coast, he'd even sold some to Eli. She had heard people talking about the large farm he had in Canada Bay. She thought about the coming winter and quickly made up her mind.

"If George Reid will have me, then I will marry him," she said.

"Don't tell one soul about this," said Thomas. "I'm going to visit George the moment I arrive back in Englee and I will immediately let you know his decision, even if I have to walk to Granfers Cove."

As Thomas was leaving, Liddy began to wonder aloud what she had committed herself and her family to. She'd never even seen George Reid. "You'll like George. He's a fine man and I know he'll like you. Don't worry about a thing," Thomas assured her.

CHAPTER
3

The Proposal

George Reid was building a cattle shed when Thomas Ellsworth lowered his sail and tied up at his wharf.

"It's got to be Thomas Ellsworth. No one else has a sail like that," said George as he began walking down the narrow path toward the wharf.

"How is the old farmer on this Saturday morning?" said Thomas as he shook hands with George.

"Never better. This is the best growing season we've ever had, even the youngsters have grown," George said with a laugh.

Thomas looked around and saw that everything on George's farm was flourishing. He could hear the sounds of sheep and goats, and not far away he could see several cows in a field. There was no doubt about it; George Reid was a very prosperous man.

"What brings you this way today, Thomas?" George asked.

"I came in the bay to see you. Got a proposition for you and want to see if you're interested," said Thomas.

George could tell something was up. Thomas Ellsworth wasn't wandering around Canada Bay for sport, especially at this busy time of year with fish to collect for David Norris all along the coast.

"Come up to the house for a cup of tea, the kettle is on," said George.

The two men went to the two-storey house not far from the water. George, like Liddy, had eight children; the youngest was seven. After they entered the house, Thomas told George he had something private to tell him.

"I don't have much time, got to get back home by noon. Mr. Norris gave me the morning off to come here."

"Yes, my son, what is it?" asked George.

"George, how are you making out here since your wife passed away?"

For a few seconds George didn't know what to say. He had never been asked that question before. He put his hands on the table and looked at them. George Reid was a man who did not talk foolishness; his conversation was always to the point.

"There must be a reason for you to ask me that question, so I would like to know what's behind it. Tell me what's on your mind, Thomas," said George as his daughter poured cups of tea and put them on the table.

"Send your daughter to the other room and I'll tell you," said Thomas. "George," he said after the daughter had left the room and George was looking at him in great curiosity. "Your wife has been gone now for more than two years. You don't have to tell me but I am sure your life is not the same. The reason I'm here is to see if you would be interested in getting married again if you found a good woman. I mean a real good woman."

George was surprised. "Get married again?"

"Yes, that's the reason I'm here," said Thomas. "I know of a good woman you could marry."

George scratched his head. "What good woman would marry George Reid. I'm a farmer stuck up here in Canada Bay, surrounded by forest with a bunch of animals, and on top of it all I have eight youngsters, so I figure the chances of a good woman marrying me are pretty slim."

"I know of a good woman who said she would marry you, and let me say she is the finest woman I've ever known."

"Now who would that be?" George asked.

"Her name is Lydia Newman and she lives in Granfers Cove."

"She was Eli Newman's wife. I knew Eli. He died last year, fell through the ice and caught pneumonia."

"Have you ever seen his wife?"

"No, but I know she was a Randell from Hooping Harbour. I knew her father well."

"I just came from Granfers Cove yesterday. We bought her fish and I found out she has only enough food to last half the winter."

"I got my doubts she'll marry me," said George. "First off, I don't think I'm any good at courting any more. I'm forty-four and take everything for granted."

"I asked her if she would marry you if you asked her," said Thomas.

George's eyes opened wide as he leaned across the table and whispered, "And what did she say?"

"She said if George Reid wanted to marry her she would. I told her I would let you know, so here I am," said Thomas.

George put sugar and milk in his tea. This was serious business. It wasn't every day someone came along proposing you marry a good woman. Thomas knew George wanted to hear more about Liddy and he decided to tell him all he knew.

"Everyone calls her Liddy. She was thirty-nine a couple of weeks ago. She is a hard worker who worked in the salting stage for Skipper Tom Randell at Little Harbour Deep all summer. She rowed there every morning with her two boys. And she is one of the best looking women I've ever seen," said Thomas.

"Does she have any children?" asked George.

"Yes, she has eight."

"Eight children, with mine, that's sixteen," George laughed, then added, "They could dig a lot of spuds in ten hours."

The two men drank their tea in silence.

"I am interested in the proposal, but how would I approach the situation?" asked George.

"I am going back to Granfers Cove in a couple of days and I could give her your answer then."

George looked up at the ceiling. This was a big decision but he knew he would have to say something now. Finally he said, "Yes, if she will marry me, I'll marry her. But she will have to live here at Old House Point. I am not a fisherman, I am a farmer."

"So I can carry the message back to her that you will marry her. When do you think you would get married?"

"Oh, right away, as soon as she's ready," George replied quickly.

"Okay, don't tell anyone about this, not even your family, until I get back to you and give you her reply," said Thomas.

George agreed. The two men shook hands as Thomas donned his cap and left. George couldn't believe he had agreed to marry someone he had never seen. "Good grief," he said, watching the sail on Thomas Ellsworth's skiff catch the wind as it headed out the bay. He thought maybe he was going insane, but then, on the other hand, he needed a wife. When George turned from the window, he saw Laura, his sixteen- year-old daughter, standing in the middle of the kitchen with a broad smile on her face.

"Why are you smiling?" he asked.

"I heard the conversation you had with Mr. Ellsworth and I'm excited, Dad. I hope you get married, you need a woman."

He made her promise not to tell anyone in case he changed his mind. Laura said he'd never yet broken a promise and she didn't think he would break this one. George had nothing more to say as he picked up his work gloves and went back to work.

CHAPTER
2

Meeting Lydia

When Thomas arrived back in Englee he went directly to the office of David Norris. He was grinning when he walked in.

"The deal is complete. George has agreed to marry Liddy as soon as they get together," he said even before David could ask him a question.

"What did you say when you first brought the matter up?" asked David.

"I asked him right away if he was interested in getting married if he could find a good woman. He said yes."

"That's wonderful. Now you have to go to Granfers Cove. Leave tomorrow morning if the weather is okay. You can collect the rest of the fish Monday. Take along plenty of food. I'll send a man with you to do the paperwork. Find out when Liddy will be ready to move to Old House Point. Get all the news you can," said David, who was just as excited about this as Thomas.

Thomas promised he would do as directed. At noon on Sunday he sailed into Granfers Cove. After he'd anchored, he went ashore to visit Liddy. She was anxious to know if he had been talking to George Reid.

"I certainly have been talking to George. I made a special trip to Canada Bay to see him," he told her.

"Do you have any good news?" she asked.

"Yes, I am loaded with good news. He agreed to marry you whenever you want. All you have to do is set the date."

"First, I want to ask you a few questions if you don't mind."

"Go ahead. I'll answer anything I can."

"What does George look like? Is he a big man? Is he tall or short? What kind of a personality does he have?"

"George is of average height, slim, a hard worker. He has a short trimmed beard. He's very pleasant and it's been said he was never angry a day in his life. He is a very tidy man. His wife is dead but his daughter keeps the house spotlessly clean. He has full and plenty. If you marry him, you will never see another hungry day."

It was quite a recommendation Thomas gave Liddy on behalf of George Reid, and she believed him. After Thomas returned to Englee, she went to Little Harbour Deep and had a private talk with Tom Randell about George. Everything she heard was good. Tom said George was a very religious man, and honest in everything he did.

Thomas Ellsworth had told Liddy he was going back to Englee around Tuesday and she was welcome to pack up her stuff and come with him then if she wanted. 'No, no, it won't be done that way," she said. "If George Reid wants me he has to come here and get me. You can tell him that."

Thomas said he would tell George what she had said.

****

George Reid was having trouble sleeping. He couldn't stop thinking about Liddy. Even when he was working her name was at the forefront of his mind. He had agreed that

Thomas could tell her he was willing to marry her, and he couldn't go back on his word now even if he wanted to. A couple of days after Thomas Ellsworth returned to Englee, Laura began to question her father about the living arrangements for the sixteen children who would be living in the house. "Where will we put them all, Dad?" she asked.

George had not thought about it. He had been concentrating instead on having a new wife. It would be like starting his life all over again, a voice inside his head told him. But he knew he would have to make plans for having another eight children under his roof. As it happened, George had another large two-storey house not far from the one he was living in. He'd built it for his oldest son Aaron who would probably get married next year. George figured he could work out some plan using this house.

"Laura," he said. "If Liddy Newman comes here with her eight children I think what we'll do is open up the new house and put you in charge. I can keep the three youngest children, Robert, Rowena and Eli, here in this house with me and Liddy can have her three youngest here as well. All the rest can be with you in the new house. You and Liddy can share the cooking, including baking bread. I understand Liddy has a daughter of about fifteen. She can be with you and help you too."

"Sounds alright to me," said Laura. "But what will happen if Liddy doesn't agree to your proposal?"

"Then there won't be a wedding, unless she has something better to offer."

Laura knew then her father would marry Liddy Newman from Granfers Cove even if the sixteen children had to sleep in the one bed with them. She turned away and

walked into the parlour, laughing. The Reids of
Roddickton and Englee are the descendants of George
Reid and, like Laura, they too are full of humour and wit.

George's older sons tried to figure out why Thomas
Ellsworth came to Old House Point and had a private
meeting with their father. They knew darn well something
was up. One joked that perhaps the two were going to rob
the merchant at Englee. Another said their father was going
to join Dr. Grenfell and become a doctor. Not one of them
entertained the idea that their father was making a deal to
marry. That would have been the last thing on their minds.
Aaron said it was the same as talking to the stove trying to
get information from his father, so they all waited to see
what was happening.

****

Thomas Ellsworth arrived back at Englee with a full
load of dry fish after what had been a successful trip. When
the vessel docked he went to see his boss. When he entered
the office it seemed David Norris was more interested in
the match-making between Liddy Newman and George
Reid than in the fish business.

"Sit down, Thomas, and tell me the news," he said,
laughing.

Thomas, who was known as a man who could spin a
yarn. couldn't wait to start. He told David every word
Liddy had said. He said he had offered to bring her to Old
House Point but she had refused, saying if George wanted
her he would have to come and get her. That made David
Norris nervous.

"You will have to be careful giving that message to
George Reid. It could well change his mind," he said.

"Don't worry about a thing, Skipper. I have the story all

figured out. George Reid will be heading to Granfers Cove as soon as I can get to Canada Bay."

"After you get the fish unloaded take your boat and sail up the bay and give him the news," said David.

Thomas assured him he would.

****

In Old House Point, Laura went outside and called to her father. "Dad, hey Dad. There's a sailing skiff coming in the bay. Looks like Thomas Ellsworth to me."

George was taking up turnips with three of his sons. They all heard Laura when she called. George put down his knife and took off his apron. "I'll be right there," he bellowed. "You keep on at the turnips, I'll be back in a few minutes," he said to the boys.

George went to the house and washed his hands then looked out the bay. "Yes, it's Thomas's boat all right," he said, "I wonder why he's coming here."

Laura laughed, "Maybe he's got Liddy and her family with him."

George didn't answer; anything was possible.

After George left the turnip garden, Aaron told his brothers they were soon going to find out why Thomas Ellsworth was coming to see their father so often.

"If he doesn't tell us we'll fill his boat full of water. All we have to do is pull out the plug while he's in the house. By the time he comes out she'll be full," said Aaron. His brothers agreed. "But first let me see if I can get some information from him. Maybe I can bluff him into telling me what's going on."

Thomas arrived at the wharf, lowered the sail, and tied up. Aaron walked out to meet him.

"You're Thomas Ellsworth," he said. "I'm Aaron,

George's oldest son." They shook hands and Aaron continued talking, "I don't think the old man is interested, he told me it was too big a chance to take, but I'll do it if you let me."

Thomas was brought to a standstill, he wasn't expecting this.

"Not interested?" he said, as he stared at Aaron.

"No, he's afraid of what might happen, and on the other hand he doesn't want to leave here."

"Listen Aaron, he doesn't have to leave here. She's willing to come here and settle down. She's waiting for him to come and get her."

Aaron started laughing. "I can't believe it," he said. "The old man is having a woman come and we didn't suspect a thing. But now that I think of it he's been strutting around the last few days like a cock rooster. Tell me who the woman is."

"I guess you bluffed me, Aaron. But I am going to leave it to your father to tell you," Thomas said as he headed for the house.

"We don't have to pull the plug, boys. The old man's already got the plug pulled. We're going to have a step-mother," roared Aaron as his brothers came running.

George watched the conversation on the wharf. He knew Thomas had told Aaron about what was going on, but he didn't care. Everyone would have to be told if the news was good.

Thomas had a story made up for George.

"Liddy wanted to come," he lied, "but she's afraid to leave her things. Someone might steal her stuff. She would like for you to come with a couple of men and help her move. Everything has to be carried on a hand-barrow."

"Does she intend to bring her belongings? Didn't you

tell her she doesn't have to bring anything?"

"She has things too good to leave behind. She can furnish that new house you have there," said Thomas.

George couldn't see how he was going to be able to spare the time to go to Granfers Cove as the vegetables had to come up. Well, maybe the boys could dig them while he was gone. It was only for one day, two at the most, he figured. But then, he thought, he would have to take the boys with him to help move Liddy's furniture.

"George, you have to tell your family what's happening. Aaron knows about it now, he conned me into telling him," said Thomas.

"Yes, I'll tell them," said George.

"Mr. Norris said I can go to Granfers Cove with you. I can bring the children and all of Liddy's things back. So, when you're ready come to Englee," said Thomas.

"I'll pay you for this," said George as he led the way to the house. He told Laura to get Thomas a cup of tea. She put a cloth on the table and brought tea and bread along with cheese and fresh butter. "We make lots of cheese and butter, we'll give you some before you go," George told Thomas.

After Thomas left, George called his family together and told them what was happening. "I'm going to marry Liddy Newman of Granfers Cove," he said. "Thursday we'll go for her and her children. I'm going to try to get David Norris's schooner and I need to take three of you boys with me."

His family could hardly believe it. Their father was marrying a woman he had never seen. They all wondered what she looked like, and so did George.

CHAPTER
5

The Trip to Granfers Cove

George would not start out on his journey to Granfers Cove on a Friday, saying it would bring him bad luck. And he had never worked an hour on Sunday in his whole life. So he decided he would start out on Monday morning. He would row to Englee, then hopefully he could hire David Norris's schooner. If not, he would go in Thomas's skiff. In the meantime, though, he and three of his sons would row to Granfers Cove. He told Laura to pack enough food for a week in case they got stuck somewhere in a gale of wind. He also told her to make sure everything in the house was spotlessly clean and there was food enough cooked for Wednesday or Thursday.

"Don't worry, Dad, I'll have everything in order when you get back. I'll even have a wedding cake," Laura said with a laugh.

Her father did not comment, he didn't think it was funny.

****

The Reids of Old House Point were well known boat builders who built small boats as well as several large schooners for the fish trade. George had built a large rowboat. It measured twenty-two feet long, six feet wide with a straight stem. It was built for three rowers and a man with an oar in the rear. George decided to row to Granfers Cove using his twenty-two foot boat. He told Aaron to give the boat a fresh coat of paint inside and out. He said they would be rowing to Granfers Cove on Monday morning. Aaron said not to worry, the boat would be trimmed and ready to go.

On Monday morning George was up early. This was going to be a very important day in his life, the day he might be acquiring a new wife. He knelt and prayed that everything would turn out fine. He got warm water, gave himself a clean shave and trimmed his sideburns and eyebrows. George was a man who always took good care of himself. After breakfast, he and his three sons were ready to cast off. They had the galley, kettle and grub-box on board the boat.

"We'll be going to Englee first to see Thomas and Mr. Norris then we'll head straight for Granfers Cove. Make sure you watch the stoves and don't let anyone touch the lamps," he told Laura.

"Don't worry about a thing, Dad. Everything will be okay here, just bring us back a step-mother," she said excitedly.

Her father said nothing as he pushed away from the wharf. Aaron was left in charge of the farm.

****

David Norris made up his mind. He was going to Granfers Cove too. David was a bachelor. He had never seen Lydia Newman, but if she was as good looking as Thomas said maybe he should marry her himself.

"George, congratulations,' he said when George Reid arrived.

"I don't know what I'm getting myself into, but I need a woman's touch around my place," said George.

"You're doing the right thing. I should have married years ago. I could have sent my wife collecting fish instead of Thomas Ellsworth. Look at the money I could have saved," David joked. "George, we have freight to go up to Hooping Harbour and Williams Port. After we deliver it we'll proceed on to Granfers Cove and get Lydia and her family."

"Thank you very much. I'll pay you for the cost."

"There won't be any cost, glad to do you a favor."

"We'll leave now," said George. "We have a safe boat and it doesn't look like there'll be much wind. We should get there in no time at all."

George's sons pulled the boat through the tickle of Englee and down through the back harbour as quickly as if they were running a race. It was close to dark when someone noticed a boat coming around the eastern point of Granfers Cove. Although the boat was small, the sight of four men in it made everyone take a second look. The boat was also traveling at what some thought was a very fast speed. George had been to Granfers Cove a couple of times before delivering fresh vegetables and butter, but that had only been touch and go. There was no money in those small places. His produce went mostly to the St. Anthony and Twillingate areas, with more going to the city of St. John's.

George arrived at a wharf in the center of the cove. He hitched his boat and got out. He wondered how he was going to approach Liddy Newman. He didn't want to surprise her by barging in unexpected, yet he knew of no other way. The only thing to do was to go to her house and introduce himself.

George Reid was not a backward man, he had entertained Dr. Grenfell and several other English doctors at his home on Old House Point. He'd also provided lodging for Mattie Mitchell and Joe Bushey, geologists and explorers for western Newfoundland. His home was a shelter for travelers, but this was a different set of circumstances. It was not just a young fellow meeting up with a girl down by the shore line, holding her hand, and chasing her home. This was a bold takeover.

"I've come to get you, so you had better be ready," he said to himself as he stood on the wharf and looked towards Liddy's house. He felt like turning and rowing back home to Old House Point. Just then a man walked out on the wharf. He had seen the boat with four people in it come in the cove.

"I'm Sam Pittman," he said as he offered his hand.

"Good to meet you. I'm George Reid."

"You're the farmer from Canada Bay."

"Yes, and these are my three sons."

Sam nodded hello. "I was telling some men here yesterday that I met you before. You gave me a sack of seed potatoes a couple of years ago when I was in Canada Harbour. You were there selling vegetables."

"I don't remember because I've given away lots of seed potatoes to different people," said George.

"You're a lucky man," said Sam. "You're getting a good woman, one of the best in Granfers Cove, and a good bunch of youngsters too."

It was now obvious the whole community knew what was taking place. "I'm happy to hear that. And now would you show us where she lives, please?" said George.

By now other people were gathering around. They all

wanted to know who the strangers were. Sam pointed to a one-storey house not far from where they were standing.

"We've been helping her pack her things. I think she's all ready to go, but I don't think you'll be taking them in that boat."

"We have a schooner coming tomorrow," said George. "She's a lucky woman."

"Sam, can the boys stay here with you while I go to Liddy's house?" asked George.

Sam agreed and George gathered his courage and headed off; wondering what was going to happen next.

****

Liddy saw the small boat when it came around the eastern point of Granfers Cove. She had been watching all afternoon. She had a feeling George Reid would be coming this evening. When she saw the boat nose its way around the point her heart started beating at a rapid pace. Lydia was a quiet person by nature. She was raised by her aunt and uncle after her mother died when she was a year old. Her relatives were old when they adopted her, but they made sure she could read and write. She got to grade six in the Royal Reader by age eighteen. At twenty, she married Eli Newman and started having a family.

Eli was a hard worker, but he never saw a ten dollar bill in his life. Although life was a struggle trying to keep food on the table and wood in the stove Eli and Lydia were happy. It broke her heart when he accidentally died.

Now she had agreed to marry a man she had never seen. Reports about him were good, yet she wondered what he looked like. "Will I like him enough to love him?" she wondered. She was nervous about meeting George in case she didn't like him. She wondered what she would say when they did meet. As she watched him approach the harbour she felt like running and hiding.

After seeing the meeting with Sam Pittman on the wharf, Liddy lit her lamp and placed it in the bracket on the wall. She sent the oldest children next door. The two youngest stayed with her. She watched intently as a tall well-built man came towards her house and knew it must be George Reid. He came up the path that was bordered by a picket fence on each side and headed straight to the front door. He hesitated for a moment then softly knocked.

A voice called from inside, "Come in, Mr. Reid."

George lifted the latch and opened the door.

The porch had a wooden floor and he noticed it was spotlessly clean. The kitchen door was open and the light on the wall made it bright. Sitting near the table with a small child in her arms was "the most beautiful woman I had ever seen," he later told David Norris. For a moment, he was lost for words. He looked and tried to smile. "Are you Lydia Newman?" he finally asked.

"Yes, and you must be Mr. Reid."

"Yes, I'm George. How do you do, Lydia?"

"So you're the man I've agreed to marry," she said as she stood up.

"And you're the woman I agreed to marry without ever seeing you," he said.

The two began laughing.

"You're more than I ever dreamed off. I thought I was going to meet a much older looking woman," George said.

"Maybe Thomas Ellsworth didn't tell you the truth," she said with a smile.

"Do you mind if I give you a hug?" he asked.

She held out her arms and welcomed him. George immediately fell in love.

Liddy told George to tell his sons to come to the house as she had supper cooked for them. "I was expecting you this evening, so I prepared a hot meal," she said. George thanked her and went to get his sons. At the wharf he met Sam Pittman again.

"Sam, can you put me up for tonight? David Norris will be here tomorrow afternoon and then we'll be leaving to go home."

"No problem. I can put the four of you up if the boys don't mind sleeping on the floor."

"No problem at all. As soon as we have supper we'll be over. Where do you live?"

Sam pointed out his house.

George went back to Lydia's with his sons and introduced them to their step-mother to be. They were more than pleased when they saw her.

"Where are the rest of your children, Lydia?" asked George.

"They went next door. I didn't want them here when you came," she said.

"We want to see them," George said.

Lydia went outside and called and in a few minutes her remaining six children arrived. George said many times they were the finest children he had ever seen.

The next morning George met most of the people in Granfers Cove. They all wished him well and said they would miss Liddy and her family. They said Liddy was a wonderful person.

In the afternoon, David and Thomas arrived in the schooner. The men in the community helped to bring Lydia's belongings aboard. David Norris seemed envious when he saw Lydia. "She's everything a woman should be," he later told Thomas Ellsworth.

****

As the schooner sailed from Granfers Cove, Lydia waved good-bye with tears running down her face. But she was happy too because she was heading for a farm at Old House Point in Canada Bay where she would enjoy every minute. Lydia went on to have two children with George and they all later moved to Englee when a school opened there. George got rid of his cattle but maintained the vegetable farm until he got too old to operate it. By that time, his children were grown and gone. George and Lydia lived a full happy life together. Their eighteen children were good citizens wherever they went.

Liddy's grandson, ninety-three-year old Jack Newman of Englee, can remember back to when he was three years old and living at Old House Point. Relatives of Lydia Newman and George Reid should make a point of contacting this fine old gentleman and recording their family history. Thank you, Jack, for allowing me to write this story about your family. I wish you well and hope you have many more years ahead.

Special Thanks

Special thanks to Iris Fillier and Alvin Sutton for helping
with editing. Junior Canning for reading and adjusting
manuscript. Rev McGonagall, records. And thanks as well to
Naaman Randell, Spurgan Randell, Robert Keefe, Wayne
Robson, George Elliott, Roger Sheppard, Bernard
McDonald, Charley Breen, George Ellsworth, Roland
Ellsworth, Carl Pilgrim, Nancy Pilgrim, Marsha Pilgrim,
Charley Ellsworth, Margaret McDonald, Wavy Andrews.

About Earl

Earl B. Pilgrim, Newfoundland and Labrador's favourite storyteller, was born in Roddickton in 1939 and still lives there with his wife Beatrice. He and his wife have four grown children.

Earl started his working career in the Canadian Army where he got involved in the sport of boxing and went on to become Canadian Light Heavyweight Boxing Champion.

Following his stint in the Army, he worked as a Forest Ranger with the Newfoundland and Labrador Forestry Department. Nine years later he became a Wildlife Protection Officer with the Newfoundland Wildlife Division.

Earl has won many awards for his work, including the Queen Elizabeth II Golden Jubilee Medal; the Safari International Award; the Gunther Behr Award; and the Achievement Beyond the Call of Duty Award.

Earl and his son, Norman, have a wilderness lodge in the mountains of the Cloud River near Roddickton. They offer big game hunting for moose, caribou and black bear in the fall and snowmobiling in the winter. During summer, guests can fish for salmon or trout. The area where the lodge is located is one of the most successful on the island for all of these endeavours.

Earl can be reached by calling 709-457-2041, cell 709-457-7071 or e-mail earl.pilgrim@nf.sympatico.ca.

Web address is www.boughwiffenoutfitters.com

Other great reads from Earl by DRC Publishing:

The Day of Varick Frissell
The untold story of a daring young
American film maker who was aboard
the SS Viking the day she sailed to her
doom from St. John's harbour.

The Sheppards are Coming
Read about the daring exploits of Brig
Bay natives Kenneth Sheppard and his
sons Tom and Carl as they defy the
law on Prohibition in their schooner
Minnie Rose-with success but not
without consequences!

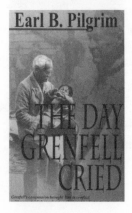

The Day Grenfell Cried
The true story of what happened
when Dr. Wilfred Grenfell helped the
poor people of northern
Newfoundland and Labrador.
Grenfell's compassion brought him
into conflict with powerful fish
merchants and almost broke his heart.

Marguerite of the Isle of Demons

An exciting true story of a French princess abandoned on a desolate island off northern Newfoundland in the 16th century. A moving fast paced story of survival against all odds by Newfoundland and Labrador's favourite storyteller.

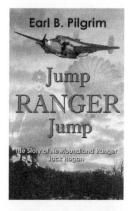

Jump Ranger Jump

In May of 1943, Newfoundland Ranger Jack Hogan was one of four men who jumped from a burning airplane over the Northern Peninsula of Newfoundland. Hogan and RAF Corporal Eric Butt were the only survivors.

Drifting Into Doom

In January 1883, Howard Blackburn, a Nova Scotia native fishing out of Gloucester, Mass, and his dory mate, Thomas Welsh, a 16-year-old from Grand Bank, NL, went adrift from their schooner Grace L. Fears while fishing off the Burgeo Banks.